# Haunting in Hartley

(Haunting Clarisse—Book 2)

## JANICE TREMAYNE

JANICE TREMAYNE

HAUNTING IN HARTLEY

Copyright © 2020 Janice Tremayne
www.janicetremayne.com
author@janicetremayne.com

First published in Australia in 2020

Cover illustration and design by Momir Borocki
(www.99designs.com.au)
Pro/99designs

All rights reserved.

No part of this publication maybe reproduced, stored in a retrieval system, or transmitted in any form by any means without the prior permission of the copyright owner.

Edited by Kristin Campbell, C&D Editing—United States
https://cdediting.weebly.com/

Published by Millport Press

Printed and bound by IngramSpark

Digital ISBN: 978-0-646-812014
Paperback ISBN: 978-0-646-81823-8

A catalogue record for this work is available from the National Library of Australia

# DEDICATION

I dedicate this book to my partner for their incredible patience—to be a good writer; you need time to yourself to achieve your literary objectives. Thank you so much.

JANICE TREMAYNE

# CONTENTS

    Acknowledgments

| | | |
|---|---|---|
| 1 | The Evil Within | 1 |
| 2 | Little Charlie | 23 |
| 3 | Paranormal Jack | 52 |
| 4 | Grimaldi's Ghost | 79 |
| 5 | Utrumque (Both of You) | 106 |
| 6 | The Basement | 139 |
| 7 | The Candidature | 163 |
| 8 | The Handmaiden | 189 |
| 9 | The Offering | 207 |
| 10 | The Cobalt Chest | 226 |
| 11 | The Vision | 246 |
| 12 | The Keeper | 259 |
| 13 | The Standoff | 271 |

JANICE TREMAYNE

## ACKNOWLEDGMENTS

Writing a novel about ghosts, the supernatural, and paranormal is one of the most significant projects I have ever committed to completing. It was different from the genre I had written before.

I want to acknowledge my partner, for their patience and tolerance for the many hours I spent in coffee shops writing my first draft.

I want to thank my book-cover designer, Momir Borocki, for designing a stunning visual cover. A book cannot reach its potential without a great editor, and I am grateful to Kristin Campbell for polishing up my work.

Although I am the author of this book, I am not a singular entity. I recognize that it was the kindness of the people around me that motivated me to complete it.

JANICE TREMAYNE

# 1 THE EVIL WITHIN

## Hartley 1936

Father Grimaldi was sent to the basement to fetch an antique cross made of eighteenth-century mahogany. It was an ornate, intricate design that was carved by a skilled artisan of the time. Nobody explained to him why they suddenly needed this cross—it had been locked away for almost a decade, out of sight and out of mind—nor did he question the purpose of it being resurrected. But it did cross his mind. He did not envisage any special religious ceremony upon which it might serve a purpose. Easter had just passed, so now was the quiet season for religious events on the calendar.

A deacon of the Catholic Church for over a decade, Father Grimaldi was never too far away from controversy—sent to the backwaters of the Australian bush for ruffling the feathers of his superiors. They had run out of patience with him in Europe, as his superior intellect regularly got him into conflicts with the conservative bishops. He was not savvy with his diplomacy, and they had had enough of his opinionated points of view. Consequently, he had been assigned to a controversial orphanage for young, deprived souls in the town of Hartley, New South Wales. And it was not any type of orphanage. This building of Georgian architecture also had its *imbroglio* and decadence—a shady past that had drawn the attention of the Church in Rome.

The poor, young children that this orphanage was empowered to secure their upbringing were the troubled youth of society, all tumbled into one great institution. Misfits, offenders, and those with learning difficulties plagued this unfortunate home for the deprived. But someone had to look after them, and so it was the Catholic Church, through God, underwritten with their care.

Saint Bernard's Church and the presbytery, built in the 1850s, was the home of the priests responsible for carrying on the word of God in this rural outpost that was one hundred and forty-eight miles north of Sydney. It was not a desired place of preference for a career priest, however.

Although Father Grimaldi was not happy with his posting, he had to endure it for the next year. The bishops thought it would serve as a time of reflection, for his personality and behaviors, and then he could return to Europe, a different man. But he was fortunate to have a sister who had migrated to New South Wales many years ago with his niece and, by a stroke of coincidence, they lived not far from Hartley. Knowing he had family nearby lessened the burden of being posted on the other side of the world.

He admired the architecture of Saint Bernard's Church and the French influence. He liked the distinctive French-style, reminiscent of his time in Europe, traveling across many French provincial towns before becoming a priest. Strangely, although he was far away from Europe, the style of Saint Bernard's made him feel at home, providing a respite that he needed.

Although it was 1936 and the church was showing signs of ageing, the solid, colonial, pale sandstone structure had stood the test of time. It had been built with a distinctive presence, like most Catholic Churches; not necessarily for practicality but to stand the test of time for the Glory of God. It had been constructed in God's name by the local stonemason, Alexander Binning, possibly one of the best stonemasons in the country at the time.

The church was named after Saint Bernard of Clairvaux, a monk and doctor of the Catholic Church. Saint Bernard had been a missionary and had opened new frontiers through his preaching of the faith in remote communities. His saint name aptly was chosen for the town of Hartley, an outpost in a new land—Australia.

Father Grimaldi was different than the long line of Irish priests who had successively occupied the presbytery since the church had officially been built in 1836. The other Irish priests had been sent to assist local Irish convicts and convert them to God's ways, to do away with their criminal pasts and forge a new living, in a new world, far away from their life of decadence. He was regarded an outsider by the other priests, and there was skepticism whether he would conform to their ways. Too outspoken and intolerant in his way of thinking. What they didn't want was an overeducated man with a degree in psychology to influence their pitiful and dreary daily existence.

With his brass skeleton key in his right hand and a gas lamp in the other, he stepped into the dark basement then descended the croaky, timber stairs. They squeaked and felt unstable beneath his feet, forcing him to lean on the ornate metal railing. This deluded underground basement had not seen visitors for years.

The foolishness of Father O'Hara to send him to a place unfrequented like the Siberian desert, to find a piece of the holy sacrament, was convoluted. It had more to do with Father O'Hara reliving the past and romancing his spirituality than anything else. But it also had an underlying mischievousness and fishy purpose.

Father Grimaldi reached the end of the pathway to a perplexing circumstance—two identically carved wooden doors on either side. They appeared to be entrances to separate rooms. No one had explained to Father Grimaldi that there would be two doors and, more importantly, which one the skeleton key would open. Was it a trick, a test, or forgetfulness on behalf of Father O'Hara?

These were not your typical doors. Built solidly with an arch-style design and carved features, they were a product of the times when doors had been designed to keep people out, bound by strength and intricate design. It did not matter if the doors were the main entrance of a marvelous house or the darkest chamber, they still needed to look good. They were bourgeois and fanciful, out of place for a room beneath a house. These doors did not belong in this dreary place.

He juggled his cape to give himself enough mobility to place the skeleton key into the mortice lock. He had chosen the left-sided door out of superstition, and nothing else. Better to start left to right was his omen and only rationale. It was like a left ear burning or a left hand palm holding bad fortune and detailed in the lines by a palm reader.

He twisted the lock several times, turning the brass key

until he finally heard the *click* of metal upon metal. His intuition had been right.

The door opened ajar sufficiently for him to create enough room to slide through. The rusting hinges showed signs of their age and screeched with a high piercing sound that penetrated the eardrums to a level of discomfort. Father Grimaldi swallowed and ground his teeth to relieve the pain from the noise.

He was inside the first room, but was it the right place?

A ravenous cellar with dark bluestone bricks hastily joined, as though the bricklayers had understood that this room was never going to be a showpiece. They had just done the job as quickly as they could then had gotten the hell out of there. The air carried a stench of dead mice, like caustic acid eating through your nostrils.

He placed a handkerchief over his face and tied it to the back of his head to filter the smells and offer relief from the putrid, stale air. Father Grimaldi then lifted his lamp to get a better view and looked across the room, seeking out the ornate cross, but the dense moisture in the air stifled his visibility.

To his right, the mellow lamplight reflected off a wine rack with around fifty bottles of red sacramental wine. These bottles, covered in dust one-inch thick, contained ageing wine used in delivering the Eucharist.

He brushed off the dirt on the wine bottle closest to him and read, *Altar wine, Tawny Port-1850. Made by Monks in New South Wales.*

Dissociated with the rest of the world above, this room lived in its own dimension, locked in time and fermenting its ideology of secrecy and reclusiveness. If the room was alive, this was how it was portrayed—nothingness, miserable, and empty of all memories. If a place could die, then this one was already dead. If life was not worth living, then it had succumbed already to superficial non-existence and misery. The sins of the past poisoned this room; Father Grimaldi could sense it, and it made his body tingle at the thought.

The chilling cold air caused him to start shaking as he was not prepared with his thin black cassock to withstand the elements. He wanted to leave and get out quickly from this wretched place.

He took a couple of steps forward, reluctantly at first, into the room to check for the ornate cross. However, it was something else that caught his attention—a cobalt blue metal chest, about knee height. It was the type of chest used by pirates to store precious cargo. How such a chest had gotten to the cellar in the first place was a mystery. It was uncommon to find such a piece in a rural town. Nevertheless, it looked new and well preserved, untouched by human hands for over a hundred years.

Father Grimaldi was cold and uncomfortable, and the brazen air filled his nostrils. Yet, even though he wanted to leave, he was not done, captivated by the beauty of the cobalt blue chest.

He moved to get closer to investigate, which was typical of Father Grimaldi—always meddling and sticking his nose in places where it was best left alone. He had a lack of self-protection and an impulsive disposition that continually engaged in a battle of wills to accomplish his point of view. To his behest, he was not frightened to tackle the hard questions and was relied upon by the church for assignments in challenging places where no priest wanted to go. And although the church hierarchy found him annoying, he was their best Mister Fix-It, the man who confronted the most testing problems.

Before Father Grimaldi took another step, he heard screeching on the wall directly in front of him. He gulped while his heart started thumping harder. It had been an ominous sound, designed to grab his attention.

He took a deep breath and held it while looking disconcertingly toward the wall. A misty haze of light captured his attention with speckles of dust forming patterns of floating particles. The incandescent light came from nowhere, as there were no windows in this room.

He lifted his lamp above shoulder height to improve his view in finding where the uncanny sound had come from when, out of nowhere, an icy hand tapped him on his right shoulder then patted him on his back. He stood frozen and tense as he gripped his hands into fists, his heart racing and eyes glued directly in front of him. He shook his shoulders more than once as a tickle went up his spine. It had a skeleton-like feel, devoid of any life or tenderness. It was the hand of a dead man, but with the metaphysical qualities to touch.

He turned around sharply to confront the phantom, almost losing his grip on the lamp, to find nothing but darkness in front of him. Was it playing games to appease itself? To control the emotions of others wary of its presence?

"They send a man of God to do their dirty work?" said the phantom in an old English accent. "Well, speak up, man of the robe ... Announce yourself!"

Father Grimaldi turned toward the voice next to the cobalt blue chest. However, the sound filled the room like an echo chamber in a stereophonic tone.

"Yes, it is I ... Father Grimaldi. And who may you be?"

"I am whatever you want me to be ... Sometimes, I am something, and other times, I'm nothing ... a transient soul, my dear Father, caught up in a sinister game of trickery by the devil."

A faint image of a phantom appeared above the chest—a bearded, middle-aged man with a vintage baker boy cap and a dark grey, double-breasted coat. The phantom was not steady, phasing in and out, but one thing was for sure: it was like looking through a glass window.

"I don't understand this game you are talking about?" said Father Grimaldi. The lamp was trembling in his right hand, and he gripped the brass skeleton key with so much zeal that it left a red imprint on the palm of his left hand.

"I am here because I have the power to see everything … before, now, and into the future. But it's seeing the future that torments my soul the most." The phantom looked toward Father Grimaldi and pointed at him. "You will not find an ornate cross here, my dear priest."

"You know why I am here?" Father Grimaldi was surprised.

"And if you think that was just good fortune, I also know why Father O'Hara sent you here … like he did with all the other priests—to cover his filthy tracks."

There was an excruciating silence, and then … "You know of Father O'Hara?"

"Oh, do I know him? More than you think. And if you thought the devil was my only embodiment, have a look at your flock where he lives behind the robe to cover up his dubious deeds."

"So, why did he send me here if there is no cross?" Father Grimaldi asked.

"I am not your advisor, my dear priest; I only tell you the way it is. He knows you are a troubled man of the Church, and he fought against your transfer to this orphanage." The phantom stood up, six-foot-tall, and transformed above the chest effortlessly, looking toward Father Grimaldi with vicious red eyes and saber-like teeth.

"I seek no quarrel with you, evil spirit. I am here because I was sent to fetch an ornate cross and will leave you be."

The phantom rattled in anger with the howl of a wolf, blowing so strongly that it elevated Father Grimaldi a foot into the air, then slammed him back onto the dusty cobblestone floor.

"Nobody leaves this den of dark souls unless I say so!" The phantom was angered by Father Grimaldi's proclamation.

The door behind Father Grimaldi slammed shut, the echoes vibrating and filling the room with a thumping *clap*. Everything shook, even the floor beneath him.

Father Grimaldi placed his hands over his ears to limit the noise. Then he got off the ground, heart racing and thumping, and dusted the grime off his cloak. Father Grimaldi did not want to show the phantom that he was intimidated by his outburst.

"So, what do you want? I assume you are seeking something from me, if you won't let me go freely."

"You are a clever man, dear priest, but don't get too ahead of yourself. Better men have tried and failed, and now they grace the fires of hell, ripped into an everlasting dance of the inferno." The dark spirit hesitated for a moment, gathering his thoughts. "I have a proposition for you, my dear priest."

"And what might that be?"

"It is foretold that on the eighth day of the eight month, you will be stricken by a mysterious illness. It will be a condition that your doctors cannot diagnose, because they are looking in the wrong place. On the eighth day, you will slip into a coma."

Father Grimaldi swallowed and clenched his hands as he stood up straight, looking directly at the phantom. "You are predicting my death? That is impossible."

"My dear priest, I don't need to predict because I already know." The phantom wavered as his apparition disappeared and reappeared again, faintly, as it struggled to maintain a consistent presence.

"On your death bed, you will beg me to save you. I do not need to do anything now. It will happen, I guarantee you. But I will ensure the good doctors find the right diagnosis to spare your life."

"And for what? What do you seek in return?" Father Grimaldi clutched the skeleton key stronger than ever before. A trickle of blood dripped from his palm and onto the pebble stone below.

"You are a man of faith and believe in the everlasting. You await your God at the gates of heaven when your body passes from the physical state to the spiritual. And like all mortal souls, you will fear death as you reach your final breath and cling to life any way you can."

"I have no fear of death. I will embrace it when my time comes, unlike your fanciful explanation." Father Grimaldi stood fast and lifted his lantern to get a better view of the apparition.

"Ha-ha … Think what you like. When your time comes, you will beg me to save your life. In return, you will become the keeper of my powers, as contained in this chest of everything before it. You will agree to release me from my life of misery in favor of your life." The spirit of dark souls pointed toward him with his right arm bending slightly. "You will live on and on, with new wisdom never imagined, wealth, power—anything you want!"

"So, you brought me here to negotiate my life with you," said Father Grimaldi. "Do you think I will trade my soul with you, a spirit of dark souls?"

"Imagine the power you will have, to foresee any future events, unlimited and only contained by your lack of imagination. You can be anyone you want to be in return. All you need is to become the keeper of the cobalt blue chest."

"You make it sound attractive, but I'm aware you spin your words like a salesman. It's the devil's work, and I won't be convinced by your enthusiasm for the benefits of this dastardly life you inherited."

Father Grimaldi's rejection angered the petulant phantom. In a split-second, the face of the spirit appeared directly before him with clown-like eyes, bolded in dark eyeliner, and a white face, with saber teeth, and the fury of a wild dog. Red droplets of blood fell from its mouth, and its tongue dangled in and out like a ferocious animal sucking its lips. His head was so close to Father Grimaldi that his pointed nose touched the priest's forehead and thick, green saliva dripped onto his cheekbone like icy-cold slime. Purplish, protruding veins covered the fearsome expression, bulging out with every taunt of anger. The smell was like rotting corpses, making Father Grimaldi cough profusely. The handkerchief that covered his face could not stop the caustic odor from penetrating his lungs.

"Do you believe me now, my dear priest? Don't mock me again, or I will unleash the strength of a hundred demons to devour your purified soul."

Father Grimaldi was a trained psychologist in the Catholic Church, and his capacity to assess character was second nature to him. He quickly determined that the phantom was a conversationalist, a lonely ghost that craved attention to amuse himself. He would continue to question him by being curious enough to create a diversion. He had to get out of the dark basement.

He walked back toward the door, each step followed by a grinding sound of sand and pebble stone, like crushing grains in a stone maze.

Feeling a pinch to his right ankle, Father Grimaldi instinctively kicked his leg, but it made no difference. A second pinch, like piercing fingernails and more profound this time, occurred to his other limb. He jolted in pain and shook his leg more than once, anticipating another bite. Something was gnawing at his ankles like a chihuahua as he continued to step back toward the safety of the door. He could feel the warm droplets of blood from his wounds slither down his skin. He was apprehensive about the phantom's motives.

The room rattled underneath him, and the cement dust between the mortar joints in the wall filled the air with a powdering dust cloud. He coughed a few times while trying to stay upright and maintain his balance. It was like standing on a train jolting over uneven and poorly maintained railway tracks.

Next to him was the old wine rack. One bottle exploded, sending glass towering over his head in a controlled manner as the wine splatted him. The stench of it filled his nostrils with a vinegar essence, having fermented over the years.

It was clear the phantom was sending a warning shot and had directed the glass out of harm's way. It was more of a show of force than anything else.

Father Grimaldi had to think quickly to prevent the phantom from his next show of force and calm him down.

"Tell me; what is in that chest?" asked Father Grimaldi.

The phantom did not respond straight away but hesitated before saying, "This chest has hidden powers that are best left alone, my dear priest. And anyway, you will soon find out what murkiness lies inside."

"I'm sure you could share an insight of what is to come. Entice me, dark spirit. You want to negotiate a deal but offer no incentive?" He looked directly at the phantom and noticed he had piqued its curiosity. The phantom loved to debate, and it was the stubborn arguments of Father Grimaldi that would draw him into a robust discussion.

The phantom halted and sat on the chest, seeming pensive and unsure of how to react next.

"Inside this chest lies a dark secret, a tool that will extenuate your ability to predict and foretell anything of desire."

"Could I foresee the winner of the next horse race at tomorrow's meet?" asked Father Grimaldi.

"Oh, a gambling priest, are you?"

"No, I just used it by way of example."

"The answer is yes, and every horse meet after that … forever and ever. You can bet on the winning horse and win handsomely, time and time again."

"I could be rich?"

"You could be more than rich, my dear priest."

"So, why are you here and why don't you live in a mansion?" asked Father Grimaldi.

He had struck a raw nerve that left the dark spirit speechless.

"For that, you will need to find out for yourself. Just like I did."

The door flung open and Father Grimaldi gingerly made his way out, albeit cautiously at first. The phantom had had enough entertainment for the day.

Father Grimaldi was so eager upon leaving the dark room that his cassock tore on the side of the door. Nevertheless, he fixed his sight on the staircase and did not look back. He wanted out of there and nothing to do with the phantom.

"Oh, and tell Father O'Hara to stop sending me men of the robe. As for you, dear priest ... I will see you on the eighth day of next month, the day of your reckoning," said the phantom with a burst of sarcasm.

The death premonition shook Father Grimaldi, so much so that he raced toward the stairs, unbeknown he had left behind the skeleton key covered in his blood.

His departure left a trail of red droplets that were sucked up by the dusty floor. He clung to the rails of the wooden staircase as he pushed his body up the flight of stairs like a mad man to the safety of the main entrance.

At the top, he threw the door shut behind him with an echoing *bang*, locking the large bolt to secure it. Then he placed his back against the wall and slowly slid down into a fetal position with both hands over his eyes, weeping painful tears.

Had he just avoided a possession by being quick on his feet and calm enough to negotiate his way out wittingly? And what about the prediction of his death that now hung over him? Eight days to go before the eight day of the eighth month ... before the truth of this prophecy would unveil.

He was a blighted man, not because he was cursed, but because he had to live with the thought of not knowing whether this insidious prediction would prove right.

Later that night, Father Grimaldi woke up in his bed with Father O'Hara seated next to him on a Chesterfield that had seen better days. It squeaked with his every movement, and his overweight body struggled against the worn-out frame.

He glanced over to Father O'Hara, unsure about the events that had led to him being in bed. "You knew there was no ornate cross. Why did you send me there to face that phantom?" Father Grimaldi turned on his side and slid his pillow underneath his shoulders to relieve the stiffness in his neck.

Father O'Hara sat reticent and looked toward him. "You are not the first priest I have sent to that wretched room to fetch an ornate cross."

"There have been others who have met the phantom?"

"Yes, it's how we appease him ... control him before he runs amok. We amuse his paltry mind and keep him distracted."

"Why didn't you tell me about him?" Father Grimaldi was incensed.

"You would not have gone if I told you the truth." Father O'Hara took hold of his cross in his right hand and said, "We are doing God's work; it's our duty to contain him."

"Contain him from what? I don't understand what you are talking about, Father."

"He has immense evil powers, passed onto him through benefactors of lies and trickery—the devil himself."

"Can you be clearer, Father?" Father Grimaldi was becoming impatient and tossed in his bed, unable to find comfort with himself.

Father O'Hara kissed his cross then tied the rosary beads around his hand. "It can foretell future events, and they can become an omen of things to come. Without controlling him, he can affect countless lives, destroying their sense of everyday reality, tear apart marriages, relationships, and turn love to hate within an instant."

"He made an offer to me."

"He did that with the other priests, also."

"And what happened?"

Father O'Hara looked across the room, avoiding eye contact. He felt the pain inside of what he was about to say. His explanation would inflict a sense of fear into Father Grimaldi. There was no way of explaining it positively.

"One priest died suddenly of a mystery illness. The other two priests went mad and were relocated to an asylum, one of which has attempted suicide more than once."

Father Grimaldi's face turned red, the anger inside him ready to explode. He could feel his heart racing rapidly. "And with all that, you still sent me down there to suffer its wrath!"

Father O'Hara lowered his head to avoid eye contact. He was fighting a losing battle. There was no way he could turn a horrible event into a positive outcome.

"We do God's work," he said. "We do God's work."

"Oh really? Is God going to save me when I die? He gave me a warning that on the eighth day of this month, I will die!" Father Grimaldi was furious that his life was at risk for some other priest who believed it was all for God's work—expendable, a sacrifice in the name of God.

"I understand your anger, my son. I feel your pain and hurt."

"So, why does God not send his angels to deal with this monster and be rid of him forever?" Father Grimaldi said.

"God does not lower himself to his level. Dealing with an evil phantom is our work. That is why you and I are here, as servants of God."

There was a deafening silence in the room as both men looked at each other silently.

With a cross in his hand, dangling from white rosary beads, Father O'Hara commenced praying. A tear rolled down his left eye as it clung to his ageing, wrinkled skin.

Father Grimaldi reached for his own cross and beads, wrapping it around his hands to join Father O'Hara in prayer.

"Hail Mary, full of grace, the Lord is with thee. Blessed are thou amongst women and blessed is the fruit of thy womb …"

## 2 LITTLE CHARLIE

Father Grimaldi woke up from a broken sleep, nervous and anxious about the day ahead. It hadn't been his only sleepless night; his poor resting patterns had plagued him since the encounter with the phantom. It had dogged his mind regularly as he awaited the truth about the warning, like a death sentence.

The phantom was an evil spirit and embroiled in a legacy of lies, trickery, and harmful behavior—it could not be trusted. Hence, the only way that Father Grimaldi was going to confirm the truth was to wait until the eighth day of the eighth month, and today was the day of reckoning. Would he break down with a mysterious illness as predicted?

As the day wore on, he felt okay, like any other day. There were no signs of anything sinister; he was the same as usual.

Walking was his passion, and he enjoyed the serenity of

the gardens surrounding the orphanage. Father Grimaldi liked to stroll in its tranquility while the children were in class. The roses were in full bloom and lined up in an orderly manner next to the pond that had a sandy track. The two-minute walk to circumnavigate the pond was just right for a man of his age. If he were feeling up to it, Father Grimaldi would walk around the pond five times.

He was cognizant of what you could see in nature when in a relaxed state. The birds, gum trees, filtered sunlight, and the smell of the Australian bush were all part of the same ecosystem. It kept him fit and provided the rare opportunity to reflect. His goal was always to come up with an idea. To find a solution to a problem that the other priests had put in the too hard basket. Father Grimaldi was a solution-orientated person who thought outside the box.

Being responsible for an orphanage of fifty children from the age of five was demanding. These children had lost their families, and some had never met their biological parents. Some had been abandoned because they had a medical condition that the parents could not afford to treat. They came from the expanses of the underprivileged and uneducated, and it was left to the Catholic Church to give these children a sense of family. The depravity of not having a parent or family meant their behaviors were always under scrutiny.

Nevertheless, all Father Grimaldi and Father O'Hara could do was ensure that God's love would pass onto the children through their charitable work. Father O'Hara would always say, "Give them all the love bestowed upon them by God. Watch them grow and let them find their place in the world." That was the motto and the measure of success for the orphanage.

For now, however, they were protected from the evil specter, and no orphan could enter the basement of the orphanage. Always locked through a series of trap doors and bolts, the children couldn't venture into that cursed room, even if they were adventurous or mischievous.

The children were oblivious of what lurked in that cellar, and for some reason, the phantom never made any attempt to cross paths with the orphans. There was only one objective—to release itself from its one hundred years of misery. His prize had to be a man of God. That was the agreement the phantom had made with the devil when it had traded its soul for the enduring powers of wealth and knowledge.

Children were no challenge for the ghost—it was too easy to conquer the mind of a child. But what a challenge to witness the servants of God succumb during a spiritual battle between good and evil.

Father Grimaldi was summoned to the office by Father O'Hara to answer a call. It was his sister, who lived in the township of Hartley Vale, five miles away from the orphanage. He briskly walked into the office, unsure what was awaiting him.

Father O'Hara stood motionless with a somber look on his face and phone in his right hand. Father Grimaldi had seen this look before, and it was not good news.

"So, what is it, Father?" asked Father Grimaldi.

They both looked at each other silently.

"It was your sister. She could not wait for you any longer and asked me to pass on a message."

"Well, what is it? Can you tell me?"

"Your niece has been struck by a mysterious illness and has been taken to the hospital in Lithgow for observation. She is very ill."

Father Grimaldi stopped in his tracks and leaned against the desk in front of him. "Oh, my God, it was supposed to be me, not her!"

"That is the way it works, Father. He is a liar and a cheat who cannot be trusted. The phantom has found another way to get your attention."

"And the premonition is true, then?" said Father Grimaldi.

"Yes, just like all the others. Although, on this occasion,

he has found something dear to you that it can use as leverage."

Father Grimaldi, furious and angry, raised his hand and pointed toward the cellar. "I will go down there now and end this insidious game!"

"Hold onto yourself, Father; you can't go there alone. It is too powerful and knows what your reaction will be." Father O'Hara placed his hands on Father Grimaldi's face and said, "Look at me! You can't just walk in there in a blaze of anger and fight it without a plan. It does not reason. You are dealing with an angry devil, encapsulated in the soul of many people."

"What about her sudden illness? How do you explain it?" He was conscious of the phantom's prophecy—eighth day of the eighth month—and questioned why he had not been affected. He understood the sorcery and trickery of the devil incarnate, having witnessed it many times before in his psychological assessments of other possessions.

Was Father Grimaldi overthinking and putting too much into it? Was it necessary to let it consume him so much? Was the mystery illness with his niece just a coincidence?

Something bothered him. It did not seem right. His experience with the phantom had been different. He rated it more powerful, astute, and manipulative, unlike he had witnessed before.

Back in Europe, Father Grimaldi had also performed psychological assessments on the faithful deemed possessed by priests. He was a frontline advocate for the Church in psychological evaluations and providing a rational explanation of demonic possessions. In most cases, it was coming up with a diagnosis that explained the behavior as a mental illness and nothing to do with evil possession. There had been the circumstance when he had been bereft of any conclusion for those deemed possessed. That was not explainable in psychological terms and open to doubt. Those had been the severe cases where the Catholic Church had authorized exorcisms instead.

The Church was aware something was not right in Hartley and at the presbytery. That had been another reason why they had sent him to investigate. His job was to get to the bottom of the strange, unresolved incidences with other priests.

Father O'Hara sensed this and was uncomfortable with his presence. It made their relationship strained and brought them into disagreements on several issues. The facts were undeniable—a priest had died of a mysterious illness, two had ended in a mental asylum, and an orphaned child had gone missing.

Saint Bernard's Church had its scruples, and the many

years of self-management in a rural backwater was taking its toll. The Church was trying to wrestle back control before Saint Bernard's became an embarrassment to the faith.

Father Grimaldi was restless, moving side to side in his hospital bed to relieve the pain, but it made no difference. It was hurting everywhere, and the doctors could offer no relief. It had started with a little pain to the side of his stomach that had grown intensely by the hour until his whole belly and upper torso was a deep red from infection. The doctors could not explain it. Test after test had proven inconclusive, and they feared his health was spiraling dangerously.

Father O'Hara, who had been by his bedside for most of the afternoon, had left temporarily to deal with a matter back at the orphanage. He would be returning later to comfort him in whichever way he could.

Father Grimaldi was all alone, unsure of what fate awaited him, continually thinking about the phantom's premonition. He looked outside the window facing directly in front of him. It was a typical four-pane sash window of the Victorian era, with colored glass that filtered light into the room in a slightly yellow haze. It was soft, warming, and peaceful.

A whisper called his name. It was so faint he held his breath for a short moment to concentrate on where it had come.

"My dear priest, it is I who calls you in your final hours of pain."

Father Grimaldi was familiar with the voice, even though he was drowsy from morphine. He recognized it as the phantom.

"What brings you here, evil spirit?"

"Oh, I am here, there, everywhere," said the phantom sarcastically. "I can be wherever I want to be, in the present or the future, I have no barriers, other than I must return to my cellar at the end of every night and to that wretched cobalt blue chest."

Father Grimaldi looked up and saw the phantom sitting on the visitor's chair directly in front of his bed. "So, what it is you want from me?"

"My dear priest, have your forgotten our previous conversation?" said the phantom. He turned toward Father Grimaldi and, within an instant, his orange, crinkled face and broken front teeth were directly in front of him. The phantom licked its lips while maintaining a fixed stare with both eyes failing to blink once. White-faced and like a clown, it accentuated the deep red, bloodshot eyes.

Startled, Father Grimaldi slanted his head slightly to the

right to avoid eye contact. The smell was putrid, like a rotting corpse. He held his mouth and nose with his hand to limit the effect of the stench.

"I will ask you again, evil spirit: what is it you want from me?"

"I have seen many men on their death beds, and I can assure you one thing remains true to all. You will cling to life for as long as you can, no matter what your belief, whether it's in God or some other relic." The phantom pointed directly at Father Grimaldi with an accentuated demeanor. "There is one thing you all think about before you perish ... It's not the bright lights of heaven and the transition to your afterlife. You will do anything for *one more day* with your family and loved ones."

Father Grimaldi looked up to the phantom and said, "So, you just want to torment me for your pleasure?"

"Oh no, my dear priest. I have a proposition for you, so listen to me carefully. You will die tonight at 4:15 a.m., but I can stop that easily and ensure your doctors find the diagnosis for your illness. I will agree to save the life of your niece, too. And, as for you, my dear priest, one more day with your family before the hour of your death." The phantom moved back to his chair in an instant and sat purposely with his legs crossed.

"You are testing my resilience ... What are you asking

for in return?" Father Grimaldi coughed each time he spoke as the pain resonated through his lungs and chest.

"You will agree to inherit my curse and set me free. You just need to say the words, and it will be done."

"How can I trust you …? You are the toil of the devil incarnate … You work for him and play his cruel games."

"Oh, dear priest, there is no need to offend me. The lies and trickery of my devil are no different than the contradictions of your church, or should I go on and on and provide you examples?"

"What are you referring to?"

"Oh, so you don't know about the missing boy—what happened to him?" The phantom laughed.

"You're referring to the missing orphan child, a six-year-old boy?"

"Oh yes, my dear priest. Perhaps your man of the flock who represents your Church in Hartley—Father O'Hara—could come clean on his disappearance."

"Why would I believe you?"

"Well, you don't have to believe me. I can tell you where this child's body rests—near the outskirts of the pond of the orphanage, buried in an unmarked grave next to the old eucalyptus tree."

Father Grimaldi choked at the thought that a priest could do such a despicable act to a child in his care.

"But how can I trust you are telling me the truth?" asked Father Grimaldi as he sought reassurance.

"You can never trust a devil; you should know better than that." The phantom smirked and said, "He was a beautiful boy; big, bright blue eyes and ash-blonde hair. He had the face of an angel, and your God did not protect him."

"I don't believe any of our priests would commit such a heinous act. Surely there must be an explanation," said Father Grimaldi as he coughed uncontrollably.

"Oh, you will believe me, dear priest, when I provide you with the exact location of the body. You can see for yourself and make your judgment."

"So, what is it you want from me …? You have been avoiding my question till now?"

"I understand your impatience, Father. Time is running out. Let me explain clearly. Imagine you have a royal flush, and that winning poker hand is me. I want to be set free and, to do so, I must appease my devil with a man worthy of a prize. You are my trophy, and he will accept it." The phantom stood up and pointed toward the next room, toward Father Grimaldi's dying niece. "Your niece is a small prize, but you are my victory against your God."

"I am your vengeance toward my God? A prized trophy for you master?"

"Yes, something like that. So, what do you say, my dear priest—save your niece, spend a day with your family, and inherit my curse? Will you become the keeper of the cobalt blue chest?"

The phantom glided toward the door like a transparent apparition, but before leaving, he turned back to Father Grimaldi. "The pain you are experiencing now is nothing like the pain you will experience in the next two hours. I will leave you now, but just say the word and I will hear you, Priest."

Father Grimaldi did not have the strength to lift his head farther above the pillow to watch the phantom leave the room.

"Oh, dear priest, as a parting word, it's your obligation to find the grave of the young boy now that you know his whereabouts." The phantom exited the room with a snigger.

A piece of paper glided into the room and floated toward him, landing on his chest. It had a map with the location of the missing boy marked in a precise location with an *X*, near the banks of the pond and just behind a dense shrub in a shallow unmarked grave.

Father O'Hara returned to the bedside of Father Grimaldi to find him in more pain than when he had left him. The illness of unknown origin had pushed deeper into his body, causing his legs to ache and swell in considerable pain. The morphine drip that ran alongside him was almost at the maximum allowable dose. In a couple of hours, it would start to become ineffective. It was a race against time for Father Grimaldi, and the only thing that remained was making a conscious decision.

Keeping his principles would mean certain death, but that would also include the passing of his niece. It wasn't just about him, but an innocent life caught between himself and the evil curse of the phantom.

"You're back again, Father O'Hara. And thank God you're here because, according to the phantom, I only have three hours left."

"Is there anything I can get you? Some water perhaps?"

"No, thank you, Father … At the moment, I can't swallow anything, let alone think about my physical state … But please, tell me what happened to the other priest?"

Father O'Hara did not respond immediately, preferring to take his time while filling his glass with water. He looked down almost in denial and said, "He passed away in hospital; did not give in to the phantom and died a tragic death."

"He preferred to die?" said Father Grimaldi. "Was it a fight until the end?"

"The phantom harassed him until his final moments."

"He was a brave man and spirited."

"Yes, but he did not have a niece hanging over him. The evil phantom has learned from his experience and become trickier. It chose you because you have a young niece who he could leverage."

"It's like having a gun against your head, holding you morally captive, except with the barrel staring you right in the eye," said Father Grimaldi with a croaky voice.

"The devil does not need to possess you to become controlling. He just needs to poison us with his venom of hatred, lust, greed, and other vices." Father O'Hara took the hand of Father Grimaldi and gently patted it. "His job is to destroy lives, our families' and communities'."

"I have always believed that is the mandate of the phantom."

"Yes, and that mandate comes with the dangling of a carrot, just like with Adam and Eve and the forbidden apple."

Father Grimaldi repeatedly coughed as his face screwed up with the tension of every breath of agony. "I can't take this any longer," he said.

"My dear father, I have seen this before with our other priest and witnessed his torturous ending. The devil will tempt you until your final moment."

"He dangles the carrot over me with the power of future visions, to use them in whichever way I want. To prosper from the power embodied by the devil ... That's the temptation he bestows upon me to save my niece and deliver me from my terrible pain."

Father O'Hara remained silent, not wanting to aggravate him anymore. In the hour of his pain and impending death, what could he say to Father Grimaldi that would bring him even the smallest of comfort? The decision belonged to Father Grimaldi, just like the priests before him.

The time was arriving for Father Grimaldi's end, and he could barely move any part of his body, absorbed in an excruciating pain that had slowly worn him down. Doctors frantically walked in and out of his room, desperate to save him, as his fragile body barely clung to life. It was his spirit and inner strength that kept him alive until now, but that also had its limits, and many in a similar condition would have given up already.

The doctor informed Father O'Hara that the other priest was not going to make it through the night and suggested this would be the time to administer the final rites. Other news had come to hand that his niece was also in her last moments and not expected to survive the night.

Was it a coincidence that Father Grimaldi and his niece had both succumbed to an unexplainable illness at the same time? Perhaps the phantom's mystical powers to predict unforeseen and unexpected outcomes was an unwavering curse, bestowed upon it as part of the evil blight—the pact with the devil unbeknown to it when tricked into a false pretense.

Father O'Hara began to administer the last rites, whispering slowly, "Though I walk in the shadow of death, I will fear no evil, for you are with me."

Father Grimaldi looked at him with the sadness of a man who had given up all hope of living and whispered, "Amen."

Father O'Hara lifted his hand and performed the sign of the cross. "The Lord Jesus says, I go to prepare a place for you, and I will come again to take you to myself." It was not the first time he had to perform the last rites under similar circumstances to his fellow priest. It was becoming all too familiar. Powerless to stop the curse himself, it had also left him mentally drained over the years.

There was a pause in the prayer, as was usual with the last rites.

Father Grimaldi appeared startled by the faint outline in the back of the room of the phantom. It had come back to test Father Grimaldi, unperturbed by his condition.

A desperately looking, grey, incandescent spirit appeared elusively, watching the last rites, but could not transcend closer—it understood the boundaries.

Father Grimaldi could sense it waiting helplessly for its moment that would free the phantom from the generational curse. Had the ghost foreseen the coming of time, knowing it was within a breath of freedom?

The deeply shaded penumbra of dark souls waited and waited patiently for the word, the signal that would free it from its eternally cursed existence. Did it sense victory and an end to its diabolical life?

The nurse from the children's ward came rushing in to speak to Father O'Hara about Father Grimaldi's niece, almost losing her balance and scrapping her cotton cardigan on the door, pulling on a fiber. With the distressed look that only a mother could empathize, she interrupted him to advise that the young girl's condition had worsened.

The shadow of the phantom had intensified out of the opportunity rather than concern for the young child.

Father Grimaldi, who was still capable of hearing voices around him, despite his condition and semi-consciousness, grasped Father O'Hara's hand and ground his teeth from the news.

Although the shadow of the phantom lurked about the room, Father O'Hara could not sense its presence. It was deliberately hiding its appearance from the only man who had nothing to lose in confronting it.

With only thirty minutes until his projected death and that of his niece, Father Grimaldi played with the thought of giving up and facing an eternity bearing the phantom's curse. Making a deal with the devil and its sponsor was his only way to save her.

"So, what say you, dear priest? Has your time arrived? Oh, did I mention she will die before you?" said the phantom.

Father Grimaldi cringed and looked toward the shadow of death, knowing he had been defeated. He took a deep breath, clasped his hands on the rail of the bed and, with an impressive roar and all the energy he could muster, exalted toward the phantom.

"Take me, you cursed being, and free my child! Take me!"

Father O'Hara, who was still issuing his final rites, was startled and looked up toward the back of the room. The phantom was making its presence felt and wanted Father O'Hara to be mindful of its being.

The phantom's shadow moved over Father Grimaldi's body with a black, transparent haze and covered him until he was no more.

A dark chill of opulent air filled the room as a reminder of the darkness that brewed within. The shadow of the phantom had passed through; the evil that embodied it transcended to another soul.

Father Grimaldi, in exchange for the life of his niece, had made a pact with the devil. He was transcending into a life of evil.

Moments later, the starry-eyed doctor came rushing into the room to advise they had found the source of the virus that had infected him. His white coat was unbuttoned and flung to the sides as he held the test results in his right hand over Father Grimaldi's face.

Apparently, initially overlooked, a laboratory test had confirmed the source of the infection as a rare disease. The doctor wanted to administer a penicillin treatment immediately to fight the infection that Father Grimaldi had so horribly endured until now. The doctor was upbeat but expressionless, focused and keen to get started quickly on treating Father Grimaldi.

The nurse came rushing in to set up the drip as an entourage of experts swaggered in behind her. The sense of urgency spread across the room. Time was critical to stop the fatal spread of the virus.

Father O'Hara held firmly onto his rosary, unsure of what to do next and surprised by the sudden change in tempo and activity. The news had come unexpectedly to him.

Unbeknownst to everyone in the room, Father Grimaldi had already made a pact with the phantom. Nevertheless, an awkward smile resonated from the positive news and the prospects that Father Grimaldi would recover from his illness.

Father O'Hara leaned forward and slightly tilted from the chair, tapping Father Grimaldi gently on the shoulder to convey the good news.

"Father, the doctor has advised they will administer penicillin to aid your recovery. They have found the source of your illness." He tapped him again gently, but this time, with a slight shake, unsure whether Father Grimaldi had heard him at all. He was falling in and out of consciousness as the excruciating pain took hold of his body.

Father Grimaldi acknowledged him and turned slightly toward the side of the bed, just enough to get a glimpse of Father O'Hara from the corner of his left eye. It was a crooked look as he struggled to move his upper body toward his direction.

"What about my niece?" he whispered, coughing at the same time. "Has she made it?"

"We are waiting on news from her doctor any moment," Father O'Hara said carefully, not wanting to sound too optimistic and raise his hopes.

Father Grimaldi took a deep breath and raised his chest, ready to respond. "You don't know what I have done, dear Father …" He coughed again and again. "I will become a cursed man for all eternity … I have abandoned my God."

Father O'Hara was not aware of the pact that the sick father had made with the phantom, so he looked at him curiously, unable to decipher the meanings in his words. "Oh, you're not feeling well, thinking about things that are not true. It's just hallucinations."

"I made a pact in exchange for her life." Father Grimaldi rolled his whole body onto his side and gazed at Father O'Hara with a piercing look. "I gave him my soul in return for her life. Now I am a cursed man, enslaved by the devil." He pushed himself forward even farther with a mighty effort and gripped onto Father O'Hara's rosary, a teardrop cascading directly onto the rosary beads below.

"In twenty-four hours, I will inherit his powers for hundreds of years." He took another deep breath, and then continued. "I will be the keeper of the cobalt chest, holder of predictions, and foster unimaginable wealth that I cannot use or enjoy—a life of eternal misery."

Stunned by the explanation that he had traded his soul

with the phantom's, Father O'Hara was speechless as he let go of the father's hand and took a step back, glazing at the broken wooden cross over his bed. "You will become the phantom of dark souls? You traded your faith in God for that monster?" said Father O'Hara.

"Yes, I will inherit its life of misery, loneliness, and desolation, and the power to foretell future events of tragedy and pain." He needed to catch his breath once more.

"You think I wanted this, Father? And all this time, you dodged its anger by remaining elusive and suppressing it while it lived within the confines of our orphanage, infecting our priests with the same pain over and over again while you did nothing."

Father O'Hara's face turned red like a ripe tomato as his blood pressure skyrocketed with his response of, "That is not true!" he said, grasping onto the only thing that gave him comfort—the rosary bead with the ornate silver cross attached to it.

"Because you knew it did not want you ... Not a desirable catch worthy to his devil master," said Father Grimaldi in a provocative way. "You were protected while you sent your priests to face its cunningness, to appease the phantom of its games, to save yourself and your position."

Father O'Hara was speechless as the veil lifted from his

secret life.

Father Grimaldi could see things that he could never have imagined before. He was looking through him, reading his thoughts, inhibitions, and dark, hidden secrets all at once with ease. The clarity bestowed upon him was incredible as the powers of the phantom embodied him with the ability to see through people and their motives.

Father Grimaldi could see through the lies, cunningness, plots, and plans within plans. You could not hide your inner thoughts from him and lead him by twisting the truth. And although he hated the prospects of being the devil's concubine, he acknowledged the power to see the current state of mind.

In the next ward, news came to hand that his niece had snapped out of the coma. With no apparent explanation, she was recovering from her illness. Father Grimaldi didn't need to be advised of her improvement. When the doctor came rushing in to give him the good news, he had already envisioned it.

"Yes, I know she is better," said Father Grimaldi with a smirk.

The doctor looked at Father O'Hara for a short moment to confirm it was true.

"How do you know?" asked the doctor curiously.

Father Grimaldi lifted himself with both arms, pushing

up from the mattress as he steadied himself in a seated position. He looked directly at the doctor and said, "Oh, I just know ... I know everything. I am here, there, everywhere. I am the past, present, and the future."

*Ding, ding, ding!*

The bell at the entrance to the presbytery repeatedly rang with vigor. Whoever was at the front door was in a hurry, a sense of urgency unusual for the general folk of Hartley.

Father O'Hara was having tea and biscuits in the front recreation room and jolted from the ecstatic sound of the chime. It was midafternoon, and he had almost fallen asleep on the turquoise armchair.

He stood up with one hand holding firmly onto the chair to support himself. His lower back had become stiff and frail and was a constant reminder of his old age.

He opened the door tentatively at first and noted a man with a long coat and deerstalker cap through the ornate stained glass.

"Can I help you, sir?" he asked.

"Good evening, Father. I am Detective Hickes from Lithgow. I was sent by our chief in Sydney to discuss a matter with you."

Father O'Hara had never liked dealing with the police

and always presented an arrogant disposition toward them. "Oh, of course, sir. Come inside to our visitors' room, just over there to your right." He pointed toward the room across the hallway entrance.

"Thank you, Father, and I am sorry to bother you without notice." Detective Hickes sat on the armchair directly opposite Father O'Hara and pulled out his pipe.

"You don't mind if I smoke?"

"Of course not. This room doubles up as our smoking room," said Father O'Hara.

"I thought priests don't smoke?"

"I wouldn't believe everything you hear, Detective. We drink wine moderately and play tennis," said Father O'Hara sarcastically.

"Well, you probably want to know why I am here. Let me explain. We received a note last week, and it came from Hartley, although we don't know who wrote it."

"Oh. How intriguing."

"Yes, Father. It contains a map and directions of the supposedly final resting place of *Little Charlie*. You remember the orphan who went missing twelve months ago from your orphanage?"

"Oh yes, how could I forget that darling little boy?" Father O'Hara looked down and shook his head. "It affected us greatly, you know."

"Yes, Father, I could imagine the trauma it caused everyone in Hartley." He lit up his pipe then took a few puffs. "We have a crew outside ready to do some digging next to the pond, near the large eucalyptus tree. I think you know the place."

"I see. And you believe the random note you received? Not a hoax from a madman, Detective Hickes?" Father O'Hara quipped.

"Well, it could be a hoax, but I won't know until I do some digging and find out." He pulled out a piece of paper and handed it to Father O'Hara. "Here is the search warrant."

"I see." Father O'Hara was starting to look pale and agitated.

"Are you unwell, Father?" asked Detective Hickes.

"I have been coming down with something and have been feeling lethargic." He lay back in his chair, crossed his legs, and smiled. "Nothing a shot of brandy won't fix."

"Oh yes, good old brandy. I always thought it to be a great elixir for many ailments. Or, at least, that's what grandfather used to say when he was around." Detective Hickes took another puff of his pipe then stood.

"Well, I better get the lads organized and start the digging."

Father O'Hara walked him to the door without saying

a word. While stepping down the stairs, he noticed a limp in the detective's right leg.

Detective Hickes turned around and said, "I was shot in the leg many years ago, in the line of duty."

Father O'Hara nodded again and did not utter a word. He was spooked by the presence of the detective, concerned that the dark secret of the presbytery might become public knowledge.

"I assume you know nothing more to add to the boy's disappearance?" asked Detective Hickes.

Father O'Hara turned his head and said, "No, nothing. Nothing at all."

Detective Hickes was always polite when dealing with his investigations, but he had a distrust for the priests of Hartley. For a small town, it consumed a lot of his time with unexplained deaths and missing persons all having a connection with the presbytery. He felt them a law onto their own, particularly with their confessional oaths—they could keep any potential criminal information secret. They stayed tightlipped and kept their dirty laundry to themselves. On the outside, they appeared perfectly functional, but on the inside, they were dysfunctional and procrastinated with their gremlins.

Detective Hickes stood by the digging, puffing on his

pipe. He paced up and down, surveying the nearby area for any clues overlooked from previous investigations.

The dig went on for nearly two hours before a cry from one of his diggers came filtering across the pond.

"We found him! He's here!" The digger coughed profusely and tightened the handkerchief around his mouth.

It was the blond hair of Little Charlie poking out of the mud, and the hand of a little boy reaching out of the sludge.

One of the diggers jumped out of the hole and vomited at the sight of Little Charlie. The other digger stood back, frozen and stone-faced, emotionless from the view of a young child who had been murdered and dumped there.

Detective Hickes jumped into the hole with the body of Little Charlie, throwing his pipe on the ground beforehand. He wanted to caress Little Charlie, knowing he was dead yet still alive in his mind.

Detective Hickes tried to tell Little Charlie it would be okay, but he couldn't. Little Charlie had been an orphan with no parents or siblings; no one to say goodbye. Little Charlie had been entrusted into the care of the priests for his upbringing, denied and cheated a promising existence.

Detective Hickes knew it was the priest who had decided his fate. He had a gut feeling, an instinct.

However, because they were a secret society, any investigation would run around in circles as they put the reputation of the Church before the law.

Detective Hickes was an eternal optimist, hoping that one day their iron-clad bonding would crack, and a priest would come clean. It was a matter of time, and only achievable by applying constant pressure—more investigations, attention to detail, and leads from the community. He was determined to lift the lid on the presbytery and their priests.

## 3 PARANORMAL JACK

## HARTLEY 2020

Harry held onto her hand with a firm grip as they made their way beyond the first gravestone. He tugged her a couple of times very gently, to no avail. She was not in the mood to go any farther.

"This place is so cold that I can hardly move my fingers. Maybe I'll head back to the Ute and meet you there," Clarisse said. She was shivering and starry-eyed from the chilled air that whisked around her.

Midnight in Hartley was hardly the place to be for any self-minded individual. Pottering around a hundred-and-fifty-year-old colonial cemetery, looking for a ghost, was not her idea of spending an evening. Clarisse could think of a hundred other places she would rather be.

"You'll be fine. There's nothing out here; just dead people from a hundred years ago," Harry said. He was his usual sarcastic self while directing the flashlight toward the faded engravings.

While the other gravestones were falling on their sides and decaying, this one was ornate and made of high-quality marble. The person who occupied this gravestone had the sponsorship of someone who could afford refined stone and the artisan to craft the scripture. The quickly covered moonlight shone off the bottom of the tomb as the gentle light bounced off around it, offering some visibility.

"This tombstone says it's in remembrance of the lost priest—Father Giorgio Grimaldi, 1936. That's interesting. They never found him?" said Harry.

"Did we come all this way to see a tombstone of a lost priest?" Clarisse was incessant on leaving. "I want to go back to the Ute. I'm freezing, shaking, and my hands are numb."

"Well, Paranormal Jack did mention in the opening of the tour that a priest had gone mad and missing in Hartley; his ghost sighted around this cemetery in an unusual sapphire haze ... something transparent."

"Like a thin mist?" Clarisse asked.

"Yeah, something like that." Harry directed his flashlight toward the grave next to it, wanting to get as much information as he could while Clarisse was still sticking around.

"Looks like another priest in the next grave—Father Francis O'Hara. He died a year later."

"And all this information is supposed to make me excited about being here?" Clarisse tugged again on Harry's hand as she gestured toward the Ute. "Can we go now?" She stood upright with one arm crossed around her middle and with a solemn expression. "I've had enough of this place."

"Okay, let's make our way back to the group ahead," Harry said. He wasn't going to push Clarisse any further.

"Wait, Harry. What's this grave?"

Harry turned the flashlight on the grave next to her. "Let's have a look."

"It says, '*Little Charlie, died of unknown circumstances. God bless his soul*'."

Harry moved closer to get a better look and said, "He was only six years old!"

"Unknown circumstances? I wonder what that means," Clarisse said inquisitively.

"He died in 1936 and was probably from the orphanage; who knows what happened to him?"

Clarisse crossed her arms and sighed. "How do you know he was an orphan? It doesn't say that."

"Usually, most graves have a departing message from loved ones, like your parents, siblings, or children—there is always some loving words."

"And his headstone says nothing?" Clarisse confirmed.

"Yes." Harry tugged on Clarisse's hand. "Come on; let's get back to the group."

Clarisse did not want to leave, saddened by the thought of Little Charlie. "It makes me feel so sad. Harry, a-six-year-old boy left this world without explanation and with nobody by his side."

"I read in the literature that the presbytery was an orphanage for boys before it was closed down suddenly by the Catholic Church." Harry thought for a while then said, "I can't remember the year it closed. I might ask Paranormal Jack."

They were falling behind the rest of the paranormal tour group that was headed by the enigmatic local ghosthunter—Paranormal Jack. His tours had become folklore in the Australian Blue Mountains and the ghost town of Hartley. The additional package of fifty dollars included visits to the old courthouse, Farmer's Inn, Saint Bernard's Church, and its adjoining cemetery. Paranormal Jack had worked out that the midnight setting of an abandoned church with the backdrop of the graveyard would be enough to send a shiver through anyone's spine.

Saint Bernard's Church had ceased their weekly church

services twenty years ago when the town had finally dwindled in residents to a handful of ageing die-hards. It was now a popular feature for weddings, due to its gorgeous setting and design. Sundays in Hartley overflowed with one wedding ceremony after another.

The cemetery mainly consisted of ex-convicts and locals from the heydays of Hartley during the 1850s and beyond. It was during a time when Hartley had been a crossover town to the goldfields farther north. Every misfit, degenerate, and desperado wanting to strike it rich had passed through Hartley with their meager belongings.

Paranormal Jack was making a roaring trade with his paranormal ghost tours and sending some customers screaming back to their cars.

The most famous of all the ghosts was that of the missing priest from the presbytery of Saint Bernard's—Father Grimaldi. Visitors on tour said they had witnessed his apparition straddling the graves of the cemetery as they recounted harrowing experiences of almost connecting with him. They felt enchanted and pulled toward him as he waved them forward invitingly to lure them to something more cynical.

As the paranormal tour moved farther away and toward the confines of Saint Bernard's, Clarisse and Harry were left alone in the dark and desolate cemetery. All they could hear were the sounds of bats in the distance and the occasional crow of a blackbird. Beyond that, it felt like civilization had passed by them.

The wind chill was not helping Clarisse as her thin, hooded top could not protect her against the elements. It was getting colder, bitterly cold, and the wind was beginning to gust, visible from the outlines of the gum trees in front of them as they swayed from the wind.

Harry heard the rattling of leaves crunching in the near distance in a sequence of heavy footsteps. A faint light appeared then disappeared as it bellowed in tandem with the gusts of wind.

"Did you see that?" Harry asked, beginning to feel spooked as he looked ahead toward the prevailing sound.

"I can see the light directly ahead, and it's faint. Is that what you are looking at?" Clarisse clasped her arms together and wrapped them around her chest.

Harry focused his flashlight toward the uninviting sound. "It's coming toward us, and it looks like an apparition." Harry lifted his flashlight higher but could not make sense of the object in front of him.

Clarisse pinched Harry on the arm, as he seemed fixated on the object. "Should we go to the Ute now?" She pinched him again. "Should we go now, Harry!" Clarisse was beginning to sense that paranormal occurrences in Hartley might have some truth to them.

He stood motionless, almost hypnotized by the oncoming light, as it circled and swayed side to side. The crunching sound of leaves became louder as the footsteps grew closer.

Harry leaned forward to get a better view of the apparition as he continued guiding the flashlight in the same direction. "I can't seem to get a fix on it, but there is something out there, toying with us."

"I'm not comfortable with this at all." Clarisse was shaking from the tension. She grabbed Harry's arm again, this time with both hands. "Harry, we are leaving *right now!*" she exclaimed.

The apparition was getting even closer. The crunching sound of leaves and footsteps was almost upon them.

The ground beneath them was soft from the autumn rains. The piles of leaves that provided their only support were creating a slippery layer that pushed their feet into the soft ground.

While tugging at Harry in a last-ditched attempt to change his focus, Clarisse let go of his arms and fell backward onto the grave of Father Grimaldi. She landed with hands directly on top of his burial place as she tried to cushion the fall. Then she looked up to see the reflection of the undistinguishable light coming off the tombstone as she blinked a few times to focus.

While trying to help Clarisse from the slippery memorial, Harry dropped his flashlight into the scrub in front of him. The flashlight was still on but shining in the wrong direction, toward the grave of Father O'Hara, so he did not have a clear view of the incoming light anymore.

Harry lost his footing under the soft ground and felt pulled in, falling onto his side, flat on the grave with his legs in the air.

As the dim light was within feet of them, the croaky sound of a male voice mixed with the wind.

They were apprehensive and gathered themselves; Clarisse tugging desperately onto Harry and shaking intensely.

"Harry, Clarisse, are you there?" It was a loud sound that echoed in the wind.

Harry looked ahead, and directly in front of him was Paranormal Jack.

"I thought I lost you guys," he said. "You shouldn't be hanging around a cemetery alone at night." Paranormal Jack was laughing as he moved his flashlight directly toward them. His white face reflected the light like a ghost.

"We didn't know who it was. Thank God it's you," Harry said.

"Look at you both cuddling together on the grave of a priest at night. Now that's a first for me."

"It's not what you're thinking, Jack. We slipped on the wet leaves—"

"Yeah, yeah, that's what they all say. Come on; let's catch up with the rest of the group ahead; they are waiting for you."

Harry and Clarisse dusted the wet leaves from their clothes, looked at each other with sighs of relief, and then followed Paranormal Jack to Saint Bernard's Church directly ahead, the next part of the tour.

"Oh, and by the way, the apparition of Father Grimaldi has been seen levitating above his grave," said Paranormal Jack.

"It says on this gravestone that his body was never found. Buried in absentia?" Harry was curious to know more as they made their way to the steps of Saint Bernard's and on firmer ground.

"Yeah, the folklore is that he went missing one day without a trace. A search party with sniffer dogs and an aboriginal tracker called Tracker Joe found no trace of him."

"That's interesting."

"Well, if you kept up with the tour instead of playing around on the tombstones, I will mention Father Grimaldi as a point of reference. Ha-ha." Paranormal Jack looked at Harry while patting his grey beard and adjusting his beanie. "There's a lot more about Father Grimaldi than what meets the eye. I have done some research on the priest since he went missing. I found some interesting things about him."

"So, this all happened here? In Hartley?"

"Yeah, but don't forget that, back in 1936, Hartley was a bustling town and many folks lived here."

Paranormal Jack pointed toward the church's French-designed doors, with its pebble stone entrance and impressive design. "The tour group is waiting inside. Next stop is Saint Bernard's, although I don't know how holy this church has been." He laughed.

Paranormal Jack was appropriately named, as he looked weird enough. His quirky sense of humor and mannerism were straight out of the Australian bush, making him an appropriate tour guide. He had the knack of keeping people intrigued, and his "one-liners" were part of his distinctive character. It created an aura of mystery about the place. It was his way of raising suspense during the tour.

Harry was smart enough to know that appearances could be deceptive, and he sensed this guy knew his stuff.

Deep-seated in his upbringing and interest in Hartley, Paranormal Jack's descendants had graced the streets of the redundant town for more than one hundred and fifty years.

He was a local breed embedded in its folklore. And even though he was a little rough around the edges with his elocution, he knew his stuff better than anyone else. It made him the only authority on the matter of the missing priest and other ghostly sightings.

It was a tour group of twenty-five people, who had all gathered near the altar of Saint Bernard's, huddled together as they waited for Paranormal Jack to unleash his next round of local ghost stories.

Harry and Clarisse positioned themselves just behind the leading group, not wanting to make their late arrival seem too obvious. They had delayed the tour for a short time to the annoyance of the enthusiasts since Paranormal Jack had gone looking for them in the cemetery.

"Come around, guys," Paranormal Jack called everyone to attention. "This next stop of the tour is the spookiest, so hold on tight as I take you on a mysterious journey of this glorious church and the Irish priests who were missioned here since 1836." He pointed toward the cemetery through the front French-style wooden doors. "There, my friends, is a mystery like no other, the story of a benevolent man of the frock, Father Giorgio Grimaldi, who went missing without a trace."

There was a shiver in the group as they all looked

endlessly into the darkness of a poorly designed cemetery with only the moonlight that peeked out from the encroaching clouds bouncing off the decrepit gravestones. A gust of wind pierced through the front doors, only to accentuate the eerie feeling.

"Over there, my friends, lies the haunting of Father Grimaldi. He is known to rise from his grave at night, a towering, eclectic figure of a transparent ghost, inviting you toward his presence. And for those skeptics who don't believe me, have a look here on my projector screen. I have captured imagery from my S-Box Ghost Scanner—a spirit box radio frequency sweep scanner and recorder for paranormal research. It's the latest technology in ghost hunting."

Everyone moved two steps closer to the screen as they witnessed the shadowy image of a priest rising from a grave, illuminated with sparks of electric current that distorted the phantom's ritual awakening.

The imagery was even more intense as the phantom pointed toward the camera, inviting them over. The ghost of Father Grimaldi was trying to communicate. It had a message, a secret to share.

"That's just special effects. I have seen that before," said one of the tourists in an impromptu manner. He was the typical skeptic that Paranormal Jack had encountered during previous tours. Therefore, Paranormal Jack was not defensive, since he got this type of cynicism a lot.

His tours consisted of two kinds of people: those who came for the knowledge and thrill of experiencing paranormal activity, and those hell-bent on dispelling his paranormal sightings as fake.

"Sir, to answer your question, I always offer skeptics a night in the cemetery to see it for themselves. I set up the infrared cameras and ghost voice box for evidence. I then let you experience the paranormal setting and make your own judgment." Paranormal Jack stood still and looked at the tour group. "Well, do I have any takers?"

Harry looked toward Clarisse with a cheeky grin. She had seen this mischievous look in his eyes before and could predict his next move.

"No, Harry, you're not going to," she whispered.

"It will be fun, Clarisse. We are in town for the next month, so we may as well have some paranormal adventure." Harry took hold of her hand. "You know this stuff is not real anyway—"

"Oh really? Is that why you fell on your backside in the cemetery? You shit yourself nice and proper."

"Oh, come on, Clarisse. I fell over because I lost my footing, not because I was scared."

"Look, Harry, you want to go on the cemetery thing,

then do it. You will probably find a way to go anyway, if I try to stop you."

The tour group caught on to the exchange of whispers and turned toward them.

Harry looked at Paranormal Jack and found him gazing at them, hoping his challenge would be accepted.

"Count me in!" Harry said with his right arm elevated in the air. He wanted to make a statement to Paranormal Jack that he was not afraid of his challenge.

Clarisse, shy from all the attention, tilted her head down. She knew very well that, when Harry was fixated, it was impossible to change his mind.

"Okay, we have two people ready to accept my challenge for cemetery night," said Paranormal Jack. He walked toward his laptop and shut down the screen projection. "That ends our tour today, and what a better place than the last stop on our agenda—Saint Bernard's Catholic Church."

"Oh, I have one more question," said Harry.

"Sure, mate. Go ahead and ask me."

"Who is Little Charlie?" Harry waited for a response.

Paranormal Jack appeared to be tongue-tied for someone with his outgoing demeanor.

"We noticed his gravestone, and it was different than everyone else—more elaborate and with a marble headstone."

Paranormal Jack stood silently for a moment as he gathered his thoughts. "You're the first person to ask me about Little Charlie, so it's unexpected." He leaned on the altar gate next to him and said, "Little Charlie was a six-year-old boy who was found in a shallow grave just behind this church by a local detective—John Hickes. After an extensive search, the perpetrator was not found. They relocated his body to this cemetery."

The tour group sighed at the thought of a little boy murdered and looked toward Harry.

"Were there any suspicions as to who murdered him?" Harry asked.

"I never mentioned the word murder." Paranormal Jack appeared irritated. "I said he was a missing child. Anyway, the detective was personally affected by what he found that the local police raised money for his grave. They paid for the marble headstone."

"He was an orphan child?" Harry asked inquisitively.

"Yes. The presbytery across the round was an orphanage until 1936 when the Catholic Church closed it down."

There were mumbles of whispers in the tour group as they came to terms with the tragedy of Little Charlie. And thanks to Harry and his curious mind, they had gained extra insight into the town of Hartley, a bang for their buck.

The tour group gave Paranormal Jack a warm round of applause, thrilled from the experience of goosebumps and rattles in the night. They then made their way to the church car park as the rain started to patter and the wind swirled and whistled its way through the church doors. It was an excellent ending to a paranormal show, courtesy of the elements.

"Oh, and by the way, if you see a headless woman on horseback as you're driving home, don't panic and keep driving."

The tour group chuckled and laughed as they made their way through the rain, dashing to their cars to make a quick getaway out of town.

Harry and Clarisse were the last ones to leave the church when Paranormal Jack called for them next to the sandstone steps.

"So, I will see ya both tomorrow at seven p.m.?" asked Paranormal Jack, excited he was back again at his hunting ground with genuine skeptics.

"Oh, not me. I'm not going." Clarisse pointed to Harry, quickly wanting to absolve herself of any thought of attending. "It was Harry's idea, not mine."

Harry smiled to reassure Clarisse, as he did not want to upset her. "It's only me, Jack … and the other guy, if he turns up."

Paranormal Jack laughed and said, "Oh, that's okay. I must have misunderstood." He put out his hand for a bone-crunching handshake with Harry, forcing him to cringe and bite his lip in pain. "Nothing like a good handshake. Good on ya, Harry. See ya tomorrow. And if you come a bit earlier, I will tell you more about the Father Grimaldi mystery as we set up."

"Yeah, we are staying in town at the presbytery, so that will be fine," Harry said. He was trying hard not to show the pain in his hand.

"Oh, and by the way, mate, the locals don't like talking about Little Charlie. That's why I leave it off my script for the tour." He patted Harry on the back. "It's a sensitive circumstance, and people were affected for a long time."

Harry did not know what to say, looking at Paranormal Jack peculiarly. He decided to leave the topic of Little Charlie alone for now.

Harry had ended up in Hartley due to his employment, an opportunity to work in the area. It had nothing to do with the paranormal elements of the historic town. His career had been becoming stale, boring, and full of routine. He would wake up at six a.m. every morning, shower, dress, and then walk briskly to the station for his thirty-minute ride to the office. After that, it was all downhill and monotonous, going over the same drawings, check, cross-check, and submit modifications. He had once thought being a telecommunications engineer would have been more exciting and prestigious, but his personality had never taken to it. He was the adventurous type and always looking outside the box. Instead, he would scrape through the day, checking drawing after drawing and validating. He had needed a change, for he was on a downward spiral to resignation.

The assignment in Hartley got him out of that stale office environment. He was the only natural choice for the job, because nobody wanted to work in a remote ghost town. Harry thrived on the opportunity to manage himself and problem solve a delicate project that was dependent on his know-how.

Hartley was at the crossroads of reinvigoration as it became a pipeline for a new mining consortium twenty miles north of the town. It had a once-thriving economic center in the eighteen hundreds and a pathway to the gold mining outside of town. Now an ambitious mining company had rediscovered a lot of gold was left behind and wanted to dig it up. New mining techniques would mean an abundance of the precious commodity was there for the taking, and the feasibility study required Harry to build a modern telecommunication network.

Harry had never been the superstitious type, while Clarisse lived amongst spiritual customs from her cultural background. It was only coincidental that he had heard about the paranormal tours from a colleague.

In 1836, when Hartley rose to prominence, it was a vital link for supplies to the goldfields. The town thrived and grew into a regional hub for those on their way to the gold rush. Hartley lost out to the railroad as it bypassed the town, which triggered the slow decline in influence. The town slowly became a ghost town then, leaving behind a beautiful church, a renovated Farmer's Inn, police station and holding cells, presbytery, and the infamous home for deprived lost souls—the orphanage. The presbytery had been transformed by a local businessman as a four-star accommodation to cater for the wedding market on weekends and was usually well booked in advance. Harry and Clarisse were residing at the renovated presbytery at the request of Harry's employer—all expenses paid.

The company also provided him with an office in the presbytery basement with all the modern mod cons. There were several rooms in the basement, as was traditional of earlier eighteenth-century design. Harry decided on the place next to the staircase for easy access. It had a small window opening, allowing for a sprinkle of sunlight in the morning. He never ventured into the other rooms—they were locked with the traditional eighteen-century style mortice locks. Untouched for hundreds of years, no one ever ventured into those rooms. They were considered unsuitable for storage, and the owner preferred to keep them locked and out of sight of her customers. Harry had asked the owner what was in the basement rooms when he had first visited his office. The response he got was a careless shrug.

"There is nothing in there; just some old stuff from the early presbytery days. One day, I will go through it," said the owner.

It had piqued Harry's curiosity, and every time he walked down the staircase to his office, he glanced at the old mortice locks and heavily graded oak doors.

Harry was busy on the project and remained focused while the thought of exploring further persevered in the back of his mind.

*One day, I will explore those rooms*, he thought.

Clarisse and Harry were having dinner at the Presbytery Inn. It was Sunday evening, and the weddings had finished. All the kerfuffle of wedding parties and guests had suddenly tapered out into a relaxed environment. Harry liked the more tranquil mood, not much for noise and confusion, preferring a laidback ambience.

The dining room that once accommodated eighty orphaned children carried a feeling of sadness. Poor lost souls without parents had once roamed this room in search of a cuddle, a kiss, or to be pampered by someone who loved them. That had not been meant to be, and those deprived young souls had grown up not understanding what it meant to be cared for by someone who loved them. A priest or a nun would teach them manners, etiquette, and about God, but what about belongingness?

Although the ornate eighteenth-century design and renovations softened the feeling of a somber and destitute life, Harry and Clarisse could sense the sadness. Imagine all those young children without parents running around and preparing for their meal under the strict authority of priests. If you thought about it too much, it sent a chill up your spine. What would a celibate priest know about loving children as if they were their own? It was an artificial upbringing for the orphaned children who probably had not known any better.

The old black and white historic photos on the wall didn't help, either. Young children with bulging eyes looked deeply into the camera. You could almost hear their thoughts and feel their pulse … *Someone love me and take me away from here.*

Clarisse and Harry sat in the dining room, staring at each other with blank looks.

*Who was going to start the conversation?* he thought.

Clarisse had not enjoyed the Paranormal Jack tour, and now she was annoyed that Harry had decided to join the cemetery tour the next day—the Paranormal Jack challenge, as she had labelled it.

"I'm not happy you decided to go on that cemetery tour tomorrow," Clarisse said. Her big, brown almond eyes made sure he paid attention.

"There's nothing to worry about—"

"Oh really?"

"I mean, it's just a bit of fun. Nothing to worry about." Harry started to caress her hand, but she immediately pulled it away.

"Did you come here to work or become a paranormal junkie?"

"Ha-ha, that's funny, Clarisse." Harry was trying to hose the whole thing down by injecting a bit of humor, but Clarisse was not buying into it.

She adjusted her posture on the chair and crossed her elegant, skinny legs while adjusting her dress. "I suppose we better order food. I haven't eaten all afternoon."

"Sounds like a good idea." Harry gazed at her as she turned her head slightly to the right to avoid eye contact.

"Look, I promise this will be the last adventure, and then I will stop that paranormal stuff after tomorrow. Last one, hey?"

Clarisse was not convinced but understood Harry had a mind of his own, a childish curiosity about things. "Okay, last one. Promise?"

"Sure, I promise. After the cemetery tour, that's it. No more ghost stories or paranormal adventures."

Clarisse smiled, although not convinced. You never knew with Harry when his curiosity would get the better of him. But, for now, she had his commitment.

"Anyway, you need to start work on your project tomorrow. Don't forget why we are here," she said.

"Yeah. You know I am thrilled to be out of that miserable office. Another week in there, and I would have gone mad."

"Was it that bad?"

"Bad is not a word I would use to describe it." Harry poured water into Clarisse's glass then filled his own. "It was like working in an old people's home. I don't think anyone had a heartbeat in that place."

"Well, this project saved you then. Away from all that, it's like you are your own boss. No one to bother you or tell you what to do."

Harry smiled. "Yeah, it's like running my own business

with my own office. Although it's in a dingy basement."

"I haven't been to your office; what's it like?"

"Oh, nothing special. It's an old storage room converted into an office," Harry said. He then signaled for the waitress to come over to take their orders.

"Tell me more. Does it have the same eerie feeling as this room?"

Harry thought about his response. "You know, when I think about, it smells a little damp when you are walking down the stairs. Otherwise, my office is pleasant enough."

"I see. So, it's not that bad?"

"I have small windows to the outside, but they are on the ceiling. It resembles those disaster movies where they are running to a cellar to take cover from a tornado."

"Oh yeah. I can picture that."

"There are two other rooms locked away with the old-style doors and locks adjacent to my office." Harry smiled. "You know those skeleton-type keys you see in horror movies with big oak doors and mortice locks?"

Clarisse waved her hands in the air. "Oh, that's creepy. I have had enough of being spooked today. Let's eat now; the waitress is coming."

"Ha-ha. You're spooked again," Harry said. He had a youthful look in his eyes, but Clarisse was in no mood for jokes.

"Your office in the basement …"

"Yes?"

"I would like to check it out. Curiosity is getting the better of me," she said.

"I know you're the superstitious type, Clarisse. There is nothing much down there." Harry placed his hand on his chin and rubbed against his manicured beard. "I can take you tomorrow afternoon, if you like?"

"Okay, let's see the old-style architecture and take a step back in time."

"Knowing you, I bet you will sense something spiritual …" Harry hesitated. "Maybe the ghost of the priest … What's his name again?"

"Grimaldi, Father Grimaldi." Clarisse smiled. It was a cheeky, innocent expression. "Are you losing your memory?"

"Oh yeah, Grimaldi. Maybe he is lurking down there, ready to pounce on unsuspecting souls."

"Stop it, Harry. That's ridiculous."

Harry and Clarisse finally ordered their meals and continued the conversation for another hour. It was hard to stop Harry once he got going on the supernatural stuff. He knew perfectly well it was a subject that would always pique her interest. So, when the conversation was not going as planned, Harry would always throw in a paranormal element into his dialogue to get the conversation back on track.

Clarisse couldn't help herself, either. She was from the Philippines, a country shrouded in superstition and old wives' tales. Superstitions went back hundreds of years in her family and had been ingrained in her upbringing. Harry understood this well and played it to his advantage, having spent significant time in her country and getting to know Clarisse. It had only been six months ago that Clarisse had left her life in Manila to come and live with Harry in Australia.

Clarisse liked Australia. Clean, laidback, and a more tolerant society, it was spacious and not overpopulated. More so, she liked the Australian countryside and uncharted ghost towns, like Hartley. She loved the character of these towns and the Englishness of the architecture and British influence. To be able to appreciate the Australian country required intuition and an appreciation of the country's history.

She never complained about going back to her native Philippines, other than missing her mother. Beyond that, she had left her old country behind for a new life.

Harry was looking forward to the cemetery paranormal experience. It was a step up and a more scientific exploration of local ghosts. Paranormal Jack was bringing all his technology to measure and capture potential ghost sightings. There was an element of fact finding and proof that made this event more enjoyable. Being able to capture a real ghost on infrared or record their sounds for review gave Harry the chills. He was hell-bent on capturing the image of another spirit and sharing in the experience.

The disturbed apparition of Father Grimaldi rising from his grave would be the highlight of his evening. Plus, Paranormal Jack had promised to share the mysterious history of Father Grimaldi and his connection with the presbytery while they stationed themselves in the cemetery grounds, waiting.

## 4 GRIMALDI'S GHOST

It was the middle of the week, and there was no one in town. Hartley was effectively a ghost town until Friday evening when the wedding parties started rolling in. Until then, Harry and Clarisse had the town to themselves. "The keys to the lodge," as Harry would put it. Except for the residential owner of the new Presbytery Inn, nobody lived within twenty miles. Only the nearest gas station managed to attract regular clientele from the main road. Besides that, the birds sang in the morning, and the evening breeze ruffled the leaves of the gum trees. That was as noisy at it got. So, if it was solitude you were after, you were in the perfect place.

Paranormal Jack was scheduled to arrive at seven p.m. to meet Harry for the cemetery challenge—an evening amongst the graves of the dead. The mission was to capture Father Grimaldi rising from his grave and pointing toward the presbytery, inviting you to come forward.

Witnesses never understood the significance of the pointing, and it became folklore in the local community. Why the presbytery? Was there a meaning to the phantom's gesture or was it paranoia? Harry was seated in a traditional thirties vintage chair at the front porch of the Presbytery Inn as he looked outwardly, waiting for Paranormal Jack to arrive. The sun was beginning to set over the luscious trees, and the wind started to develop a chill as it picked up the cool southern breeze. It was a place to have afternoon tea while boasting a perfect view of the town and its main street. Harry was able to see everyone coming in and out of the main road from his ideal perch.

The presbytery was located on a hill overlooking the town. It was level with the church and on the same allotment. The Catholic Church had chosen this spot, ensuring everyone in Hartley could see it from any angle, as it was meant to be a constant reminder of their power and influence.

The residents were mainly of Irish descent and superstitious. The Church gave them the confidence and strength to live out their daily lives and struggles without fear. They were in God's hands. The imported Irish priests that maintained the parish made sure of it, acting as the equivalent of modern-day advisors and spiritual counsellors to a naïve audience of the faithful.

Harry had nearly dozed off with his eyes half-shut when awakened by the noise of a revved-up vehicle in the distance. He was familiar with the sound of modified engines and particularly locally built Holden cars.

He shook his head gently and looked ahead to see a dark green utility speeding into town. The vehicle screeched around the corner and into the main street, heading directly toward the church.

Harry blinked a few times, realizing it was Paranormal Jack on time for the evening's paranormal challenge. He had all the ghostbusting hi-tech systems that he boasted about during his paranormal tours.

The loud music coming from the upgraded speaker system signaled his arrival to the famous tune of an eighties Australian classic song. Harry liked it and smiled as the music got louder when his Ute turned into the main driveway of the church.

Harry briskly made his way to the church's entrance to greet Paranormal Jack and to see if he needed a hand unloading the equipment. He waved to him as he got closer to acknowledge Paranormal Jack's arrival in town.

Wearing his trademark black tee-shirt with the inscription *Paranormal Jack* and a cross on the back, he made his way toward Harry and shook his hand with a firm grip.

"Don't worry about the other guy. He chickened out, so it's just you and me," said Paranormal Jack.

"Sometimes, they are all talk." Harry pointed to the Ute. "Do you need a hand unloading?"

"Thanks for the offer. I have some pretty heavy shit in there, so a helping hand would be great." Paranormal Jack removed the black canopy and stepped into the Ute. "I was hoping the other guy was going to be here to help me unload. I was supposed to pick him up on the way, but he cancelled at the last minute."

"It's a cool Ford Falcon Ute you have here."

"Spent too much money on it. Nearly got me broke. But don't say anything to anyone. I love my beast of a car."

"You're not the first or last person to get in trouble with their cash flow over a car, ha-ha," Harry said with a smirk.

"Help me move these laser grid devices to the cemetery and into the right locations. Oh, and be gentle because it's delicate equipment."

"Do these devices work?" Harry was becoming a skeptic again.

"Yes, mate. They help to visualize anomalies as they occur in a location, such as determining speed, dimensions, and even help us make a 3D model of the entity. Once they are in place from both sides of the grave, they will detect any unusual movement hidden from the human eye. And yes, before you quiz me, I have used them before, but not in Hartley."

"And what about these voice detecting devices?" Harry pointed to the large cucumber shape microphones sitting on a tripod stand in the Ute.

"Now, that is the latest in technology, and they cost a lot of money. Did you know ghost can emit sounds at a frequency undetectable to the human ear?"

"I had no idea, Jack."

"It's called a *Spirit Box*—a great compact tool for attempting communication with paranormal entities. It uses radio frequency sweeps to generate white noise, which theories suggest give some entities the energy they need to be heard. When this occurs, you will sometimes hear voices or sounds coming through the static in an attempt to communicate."

"You really know your stuff, and it's very hi-tech."

"That's part of their frustration—they are trying to communicate and don't realize we can't hear them, so they get frustrated and angry."

"Like having a temper tantrum?" Harry was becoming curious.

"That's right. Some get so angry that they do stupid things to get your attention." Paranormal Jack pointed to the spot where the audio equipment should be located, about ten feet from the grave of Father Grimaldi.

"I suppose, after all this heavy lifting, we can have a drink on the porch and talk about the history of Father Grimaldi?"

"You are very inquisitive, Harry. I like that." He winked at him. "Sure, mate, I have some history about this place that will give you goosebumps."

Harry smiled and nodded.

Paranormal Jack got the impression that Harry was not taking this seriously and that it was a sideshow. It was not the first time he had encountered skeptics like Harry who thought it was a fun night out.

Paranormal Jack described the cemetery as one of the creepiest he had ever experienced during the paranormal tour, but most tourist thought it was part of the show and made nothing of it. However, there were elements in this cemetery that made it different from others in the area. It had a documented history of people laid to rest who had gone mad or mysteriously went missing. It was an iconic church with a presbytery and an orphanage of deprived young souls. Hartley was ripe for a thriller or whodunit as the main characters involved Irish priests from one hundred and fifty years ago.

The numerous sighting of ghosts just added to the paranormal aspects that put Hartley back on the tourist map. It had festered as a decaying ghost town for many years. Hartley had made a comeback, but for all the wrong reasons, and its only saving grace were the entrepreneurial weddings that were booked out six months in advance. That gave Hartley some legitimacy, and it brought the people back.

Harry and Paranormal Jack sat on the porch as they shared a cup of the local tea—another marketing idea in local produce that included honey, jam, and a traditional local bakery.

"So, Jack, tell me about Father Grimaldi. What have you uncovered about him?" said Harry.

"According to the local archives, I have found an interesting story—a disappearance that local police were unable to solve."

"He disappeared just like that?"

"It appears so. They used a local indigenous tracker by the name of Tracker Joe, dogs, and a local search party. Not a trace, nothing."

"That's a real mystery—unsolved disappearance of a prominent priest." Harry took a sip of his tea. "So, what keeps you interested in the folklore? Are you a local?"

"You ask a lot of questions, Harry. Not sure how open-minded you are about the paranormal, but you are certainly inquisitive." Paranormal Jack pointed toward the cemetery, which was only fifty feet from the Presbytery Inn, and said, "It will be cold tonight, so rug up. Also, don't wear any jewelry, as it interferes with the full spectrum POV camera. Otherwise, we are ready!"

"Sure, I can manage that." Harry smiled with a cheeky, childish grin.

"Oh, and by the way, my grandfather was the senior constable in Hartley when it happened. I suppose I became intrigued in the disappearance of Father Grimaldi in my teenage years."

Harry had a stark look of surprise on his face. "Wow, you're entrenched in the whole thing. I mean, it's a real insider view of what happened."

"Yeah, mate, but I don't think my grandfather told me everything. Some things unnerved him, and he would not elaborate. I guess he took some things to the grave, and I will never know."

"So, there's more to the story?" Harry wanted to know more.

"I found out that, in 1836, there was another disappearance—a ship's captain that was one of the early settlers." Paranormal Jack took the spare chair and placed his feet on it. "He was visiting his son, who was digging for gold not far from here. Hartley was the main supply town for the goldfields back then and a thriving town."

"I guess it's not a coincidence?" Harry said. His forehead creased from the intense concentration, and his demeanor was becoming more serious.

"Other than the disappearances are one hundred years apart? It's hard to say if the circumstances were the same. There was no trace of him, and the mystery was never solved."

"You are a real wealth of knowledge, Jack, and I'm looking forward to our cemetery experience. Should be a cracker."

"Ha-ha. Don't get excited too quickly, Harry. You may end up leaving this cemetery screaming." Paranormal Jack gulped what was left in his tea then wiped his mouth with his hand. "Better get started setting up. See you in half an hour, then?"

"Where should I meet you?"

"At the steps of the church. We have a good view of the cemetery from there.

Night had descended on Hartley, and not a soul was in sight. If you closed your eyes and just pondered for a while, you would have thought you were the only person alive. The few lampposts in the center of town were the only single markers of civilization. *Well, the lights and electricity are still on, so there must be a pulse somewhere?* Harry thought.

The night was pitch dark as the clouds descended over the town. The moon occasionally made an appearance, and when it did, it glowed like a giant lamppost in the sky. There was a mild breeze with a chill typical for the time of year, as the climate transitioned into autumn. Hartley was in the high country, a perfect environment for the southeasterly breeze to straddle its strips and rip across the ranges.

Harry crossed his arms and put on his hooded fleece jacket that had seen better days, grateful for the tip by Paranormal Jack to put on something warm. It was not the fashion statement expected by someone of his age group. It could have been grandpa's fleece jacket as far as Harry was concerned, but it did not bother him. It wasn't about looking good; it was about proving his skeptical viewpoint. He wanted to show the futility of trying to catch a ghost in the cemetery and what a stupid idea it was.

"So, how long to wait here in this cold, miserable place for a ghost to appear?" Harry asked. He was trembling while gripping his hoodie to stop the wind from blowing it open.

"Let's give it up to two to three hours, and if the cold gets too much, we can call it quits." Paranormal Jack sat back in his foldable picnic chair and crossed his legs.

"Maybe to kill off some time, I can tell you more about the story of Father Grimaldi, if you're interested?"

"Oh yes, I am interested all right. Give me warts and all. I want to know everything." The story of Father Grimaldi had captured Harry's imagination, and he was intrigued by the folklore.

"Okay. You asked for it, Harry." Paranormal Jack gathered his thoughts. He wanted Harry shitting himself right from the start.

"Come on, Jack. I'm waiting for it," Harry said impatiently.

"Father Grimaldi was not your typical Catholic priest from Ireland. Unlike the other priests who were more insular in their views, he had traveled throughout Europe and was a mover and shaker for the church. When things got a little out of control in a parish, they would send Father Grimaldi to do an assessment."

"So, he was not your average priest?"

"No, not at all. There had been rumors of a priest in Hartley suddenly disappearing without a trace and the other two going insane. The Church could not understand the circumstances—foul play, a corrupt presbytery, or—"

"Or the devil?" Harry replied, interrupting Paranormal Jack.

Paranormal Jack went silent, caught by surprise. Then

he said, "Yes, the devil in his playground. The orphanage of deprived young souls, as they labelled it at the time. This place was at risk of being infected by the devil's hand. Sixty young children under the age of ten were living here, and the Church feared they could become the devil's concubines." Paranormal Jack pointed toward the orphanage, which had become the mainstay of visitors to Hartley.

"What about the orphanage, Jack?"

"It was rumored that the priests were aware of the evil that resided within. To safeguard their flock of orphans, they made a pact with the demon; appeased it and kept it at bay."

"So, something evil was residing in the orphanage? Surely, you can't expect me to believe that?" Harry laughed and rolled back in his picnic chair, almost falling on his backside.

"Well, as far as the Church was concerned, it was serious enough to send Father Grimaldi to investigate it."

"So, what happened next?" said Harry impatiently.

"The folklore is that Father Grimaldi didn't go missing and that he made a pact with the devil."

"A tradeoff?"

"You catch on quickly, Harry. Yes, you could call it a tradeoff."

"Oh, that's bullshit, Jack. Never heard so much nonsense before. But I got to hand it to you, you're a great storyteller, so tell me more."

"Come on, Harry; never rush a good story." Paranormal Jack took a sip of his tea then placed the cup on the floor in front of him.

"Well, come on; tell me more?"

"I found a hospital record that Father Grimaldi and his niece became ill with a life-threatening disease at the same time."

"You're kidding? You have a copy of his medical records?" Harry smiled. "You're niftier than I thought."

"Yes, and they suddenly became well again. Doctors could not explain their immaculate recovery. They were dumbfounded."

"So, what happened after that?" Curiosity was getting the best of Harry. He was enraptured by the story, more than what he had expected.

"They left the hospital, and his niece went back to living a normal life. But Father Grimaldi was never seen again, disappeared without a trace."

"He disappeared like the other priest in Hartley?"

"Yeah … the circumstances almost identical. Missing without a trace."

"So, what's your take on it, Jack? I get the feeling you

have a theory on this one, an opinion?"

"I think this is where the story ends," Jack said, feeling uncomfortable to take the story any further.

"You started the story, you got me intrigued, and now you don't want to give me the ending? Come on, Jack; you're Mr. Paranormal—you can tell me about your theory."

Paranormal Jack felt he had gone too far and had compromised himself by Harry's enthusiasm. There was a dark secret in his tale, and he didn't want to go into it. But Harry didn't care, pushing him to elaborate.

"Oh, all right, Harry. The church's report from the local diocese says he made a pact with the devil."

"What sort of pact?"

Paranormal Jack's eyes were fixed on Harry. It was more than a stare. "He traded his soul and became the devil himself."

"What! Are you serious? He traded his soul and became possessed?"

"Oh, I am very serious, and I have the Church records to prove it."

There was a moment of silence as both Harry and Paranormal Jack reflected on their conversation. Harry realized he had pushed Paranormal Jack far enough on the folklore and decided to pull back. He had managed to extract enough information for one day.

A couple of hours had passed, and besides the occasional chat, Paranormal Jack continued monitoring his laptop for evidence of ghosts—the spirit of Father Grimaldi rising from the grave. Harry dozed off intermittently as he struggled to keep his eyes open.

*Beep, beep, beep.*

A sudden alert signaled from the laptop.

Paranormal Jack grabbed his wireless mouse instinctively, like a fisherman seizing a suddenly struck line. It was like catching a fish, and the exhilaration was no different.

In the same moment, Harry woke fully from his light sleep and looked toward the computer screen as red, pulsating signals pointed toward the location of Father Grimaldi's grave.

"Is there something out there?" Harry asked. His speech was slurred, but his mind was already as sharp as before.

"Oh, you're awake, Harry. For one moment there, I thought you were out cold for the night." Paranormal Jack grinned at him.

"Well, are we onto something, Jack?"

Paranormal Jack pointed to the red flashing markers on his laptop and said, "See these pointers here? They are a strong signal of an unknown entity. It's picking up paranormal behavior."

"So, what is the difference between the different colored markers?" asked Harry.

"I like your inquiring mind, Harry." Paranormal Jack handed Harry a freshly made hot tea with milk. "A yellow signal identifies a mouse, a bat, or a large insect. The infrared detector can measure density and heat."

"That's pretty smart technology. I'm impressed."

"There have been a lot of advancements in the last couple of years, you know, to eliminate the skeptics like yourself."

Harry and Paranormal Jack both smiled. Harry was a full-blown skeptic and a testy one, questioning anything.

"So, what do you see now? The red signal is becoming more intense."

"Wait for it, Harry. I'm onto something. This is good."

Harry pointed toward the grave of Father Grimaldi, but all he could see was pitch black. In the meantime, the infrared system was detecting unusual manifestations. "I can't see anything out there, Jack."

"And you won't, because ghosts don't always show themselves like in the movies. These entities move around undetected, and only our technology can capture their movements or presence."

"You mean, he could be standing right next to me, right now."

"Yeah, theoretically, he could. But my computer would be going crazy, so don't worry."

Paranormal Jack was fixated on his laptop screen, and then switched on the monitor display for a better view.

"Oh, my goodness, I think we have him. Look here."

They both looked at the forty-inch monitor with higher resolution. The outline of a man in priest clothing rose steadily from the grave. It resembled small electrical pulses with cobalt blue reflections of light. There was a static charge released around the ghost. It appeared to be a reaction to the environment.

Harry glimpsed toward the grave of Father Grimaldi and pinched himself in the leg to make sure it was not a dream. Father Grimaldi was rising from the grave.

"He's looking toward us!" said Paranormal Jack.

"What? You're kidding me?"

"To be more precise, his looking directly at *you*, if I'm not mistaken."

Harry peered into the monitor more carefully this time and, to his astonishment, Father Grimaldi was looking directly at him.

There was static coming from the speaker that Paranormal Jack had set up to record wayward ghost sounds—cries of pain, screams, and words in languages never heard before.

"What's that static sound coming from the speakers?" Harry asked.

Paranormal Jack raised the volume and put on his noise-cancelling headset. "It's trying to tell us something."

"It's pointing at the presbytery," said Harry, his voice cracking from the suspense as he looked on intensely, glued to the monitor.

Across the cemetery and toward the side of the presbytery, a light flickered from the basement windows. It was uncanny, as no one was staying there. The basement was Harry's office, and nobody had access to the room. *Flicker, flicker, flicker*, it continued that way for almost a minute while the ghost continued pointing toward it fervently.

Harry was getting chills and goosebumps through his arms and neck. He twitched from the fear of the unknown. He had not been expecting this, had been counting on the night being a total flop. His knees started to tremble as he shook them repeatedly to release the anxiety.

Paranormal Jack was as cool as a cat. Nothing fazed him. He was in the paranormal game, and events like these spurred him on.

Paranormal Jack raised his arm and threw his fist in the

air. "I got it! I got it!"

"Got what?" Harry was confused.

"I managed to record the message and make some sense of it." Paranormal Jack took off his headset and looked at Harry directly in the eyes. It was a somber expression, and not atypical of his personality.

"Well, tell me." Harry repeated, "Tell me."

"It's not good, Harry, and I need to verify it tomorrow."

"What do you mean *it's not good*? Can you explain?"

"The ghost was pointing at both of us, and it was mumbling words, trying to communicate."

"I was caught up looking at the basement lights and didn't notice."

Harry looked toward the monitor. The infrared imaging was no longer detecting any movement. The red pulsating markers had ceased flashing.

*Did Father Grimaldi return to his shallow grave? Was his objective to deliver a message? But what message? Was it good or bad?* Thoughts raced through Harry's head.

"We are done for tonight, Harry. Tomorrow, I will review the ghost message with my sound editing software and decipher it."

Paranormal Jack was ready to disconnect his equipment when the systems started reactivating again, rebooting. The red pulsating markers were back on the laptop, brighter and louder than before, flickering faster this time. The screen monitor was hissing with interference, and the speakers were pulsating screeching cat-like sounds. Paranormal Jack and Harry jolted unexpectedly.

The equipment could not keep up with the levels of detection all at once. The ghost of Father Grimaldi was strong and powerful, wanting to make its presence felt. It was making a statement that it did not like being messed with.

"The signal is moving toward us very quickly," said Paranormal Jack.

"You mean, he's coming straight for me?" Harry put his hands over his head as he tried to use his hoodie to hide from the presence of the apparition.

"Ten meters away ... It's just ahead of you at the first gravestone," said Paranormal Jack.

A cold, icy wind blew across their shoulders, and the air turned foul, a putrid smell like rotting meat and arsenic combined filled the air.

Harry covered his nose with his shirt, but it provided little relief.

"It's five meters away, directly ahead of you," said Paranormal Jack.

The glimpses of moonlight disappeared from the sky as dark clouds covered its beam. The church's wooden oak door behind them slammed shut, making a massive *bang* that reverberated across the cemetery, echoing more than once.

They both closed their eyes and looked down, waiting for the ghost of Father Grimaldi to be upon them, unsure of what evil awaited them.

Then, as quickly as it had restarted, the equipment turned off again. The monitors turned black, and the sound ceased all at once.

Harry felt an icy-cold hand slide along the back of his neck. He jolted and turned immediately to confront the apparition. He was so tense that he clasped his hands into fists, ready to confront the evil.

Right in front of him was the glassy face of death, a crisp, white image with bloodshot eyes and deep green irises fixated on him. Sharp teeth extended beyond the curvature of the mouth as grueling slime leaked down the sides and onto the chin. A pointed nose with creases along the forehead flashed in front of Harry for five seconds before the evil wraith disappeared.

Harry was shaking, not understanding what he had just encountered. It had been an eye-opening experience for the cocky skeptic who had thought the evening in the cemetery would resemble a *Ghostbusters* episode. It had meant to bring some fun to this boring town and break the monotony.

They both stared at each other, waiting for someone to say the first word. But Harry was speechless and exhibiting signs of fright—staring into night, silent, distraught, shaken by the image of evil.

Father Grimaldi had been in his face, a confronting and powerful depiction. It was enough to cause him intermittent flashbacks that he would experience over the coming days. He could not get that picture of evil out of his head, stuck in the frontal lobe of his brain like a black and white snapshot. His mind would not let go.

"Okay, Jack … I think we are both tired, and I'm going to get some sleep. Oh, and by the way, I will check the door to the basement tonight and see if it's locked on my way back. I'm curious about the lights coming from there."

"Sure, mate. Let me know if you find anything unusual," said Paranormal Jack.

"I am the only one besides the caretaker who has the key," said Harry. He hesitated for a moment, looking directly at Paranormal Jack.

"What's up, Harry? You look shaken," said Paranormal Jack.

"I want to ask you something … That wasn't real, was it?"

"If you are alluding that I created this scene, think

again. How could I have changed the atmospheric conditions? I'm not God."

"No, that's not what I meant, Jack ... I wanted to ask if you have ever encountered a situation like this before?"

"Harry, I have seen some spooky shit in my life, but I felt something very different this time."

"Like what?"

"It stunk of evil ... pure evil of the worst kind." Paranormal Jack packed the speakers into the metal box to release the tension in his bones. "Not sure it's something I want to mess around with anymore."

"Should we meet tomorrow for breakfast and go through the recording?" Harry asked.

"Do you want to know what it said?" Paranormal Jack had a worried look on his face. "You know, Harry, some things are best left alone."

"No, I insist. I want to know," said Harry in a resolute manner.

"Okay, your choice. But don't say I didn't warn you. Tomorrow, we will verify the message after breakfast."

"Nine a.m., then, at the presbytery restaurant?"

"Sure, Harry. Help me pack up the equipment and load it onto the Ute before we turn in for the night."

They would have to traverse the cemetery to load up the equipment into the Ute. Considering what had taken place, Paranormal Jack decided to move his vehicle across the pathway to the front of Saint Bernard's Church. Nobody was in the frame of mind to carry equipment across the graveyard.

Harry gingerly walked back to the Presbytery Inn in search of a good night's sleep. He was feeling jittery and anxious after the experience in the cemetery, which had not been what he had expected.

Flashbacks of the horrible demon-like face of Father Grimaldi projected across his mind as a constant reminder that he had been affected. If Father Grimaldi had planned to scare the living daylights out of Harry, then he had succeeded.

Hartley only had three lampposts in the whole town, so night was usually pitch dark. Harry stumbled and slid over the soft, leafy ground, unable to get his footing right. A howling wind started to take shape, and a spirited cry from the nocturnal bats in the vicinity did not help his confidence. He wanted to get back to his room quickly and leave behind the cemetery challenge experience.

While only ten feet from the entrance to the presbytery, he glanced over at the basement windows next to his study. There was a pulsating neon light coming directly from there.

He stopped in his tracks and focused again, waiting for the next pulse to appear. It was as though someone was deliberately playing with him and indulging in his reaction.

Harry was still fascinated with the light that he had witnessed from the cemetery. He was determined on a quick inspection before heading to his room. He was going to have trouble falling asleep after all the excitement and needed to do something to relax him, to take his mind off that devilish image that had become implanted in his mind.

The flashing lights made him more anxious as he picked up the pace toward the staircase leading down to the basement. As he got closer to the winding, spiral staircase entrance, he could see the intermittent flashes of light, filtering out from underneath the gap of the door. He stopped in front of the carved oak door and placed his key in the mortice lock. Shaking from the jitters, he dropped the keys onto the dusty floor, only to pick them up again clumsily.

Harry tried once more to open the mortice lock by turning the old-style key twice. *Click, click.* He thrust the door open as a knee-jerk reaction.

The door thumped against the wall from the force and rebounded back into Harry's shoulders. He lost his balance and fell onto his back with his feet in the air. Harry picked himself up and rushed down the stairs to the source of the light. He was so eager to explore the phenomena that he skipped a couple of steps and almost lost his footing, gripping the railing as a counter support. The flashing lights were emitting from one of the basement rooms that he had no access to. *Flicker, flicker, flicker.*

There were no weird noises to add to the light display and only the cold, chilly air. He could see his warm breath mix with the cold temperature with every exhale. Harry knew he could not access the room displaying the intermittent light. He would need the caretaker to let him in, and it was not an option at two a.m. Harry needed to get the key to the basement room and come back the next day.

He left the basement, unknowing of what lay ahead. The adrenaline rush was starting to fade as fatigue set in. He was tired, drained, and his concentration levels were beginning to fray.

Somehow, his encounter with Father Grimaldi's ghost had led him to a basement room adjacent to his office. He didn't want to jump to conclusions as the rational thought process kicked in again. The lights could be a faulty electrical problem in the room, and it had been pure coincidence. Nevertheless, he wanted to check it out and make sure there was a logical explanation. For now, that would have to wait until the next day.

# 5 UTRUMQUE (BOTH OF YOU)

It was Friday in Hartley, and usually, the entourage would start rolling in for the wedding ceremonies at Saint Bernard's Church. It was becoming so popular that they scheduled the services every two hours, enough time to get one wedding party in, married and out, and ready for the next one. After each ceremony, there were light drinks and refreshments at the presbytery dining room, once frequented by Irish priests over one hundred and fifty years ago.

Black and white photos of Saint Bernard's Church and the presbytery faithful covered the dining room foyer to remind guests of the rich history of Hartley. The young, fresh faces of the priests, some happy and some benign, provided a characterization of what life had been like in this Catholic outpost. They were young priests sent to a new land without choice, to preach the virtues of being a good Catholic amongst a flock of transient souls.

For now, the dining room was empty, and only Clarisse and Harry presented themselves for breakfast. Being the only people in a large room gave them all the privacy and attention they needed, but it also gave a sense of being in the middle of nowhere. You could become lonely here or foster the richness of solace and serenity. It depended on what you were seeking.

"You got in very late last night, Harry. How did it go? Did you catch your ghost?" Clarisse giggled.

Harry stalled the discussion by filling his mug with percolated coffee. "We sort of did and didn't."

"What is that supposed to mean?"

"Well ... when you consider all the equipment Jack had laid out in the cemetery—"

"Like the movie *Ghostbusters*?" Clarisse interjected.

Harry smiled and shifted in his chair, tapping on the table nervously. "Jack reckons he got a recording of something."

"And? I'm assuming it's a ghost; maybe that of Father Grimaldi?"

"Not sure what it was because he didn't elaborate too much, but he looked spooked." Harry took a sip of his coffee while looking out the window and into the main street. "He should be joining us soon for breakfast with the recording. I guess we are going to find out."

"Hey, that sounds creepy," she said, glancing to the coffee plunger. "Do you think I can have some coffee, too, before you drop the whole thing on the table?"

"Oh, sorry about that. Still tired from yesterday. I didn't sleep that well last night."

"So, that's it? Five hours in a cemetery and all you have is a recording?" Clarisse nodded and smirked. "You know that recording could be anything. There are lots of nocturnal animals roaming that cemetery at night."

"Yeah, it is a rural town, and there are many animals around here; little ones in particular that you can't see." Harry put down his coffee cup and glanced at Clarisse.

"What's that look, Harry? Something's bugging you. What is it?"

"Paranormal Jack said he never heard a recording like that before, and he seemed bothered."

"Paranormal Jack, the ghost hunter and paranormal tour guide, spooked? You're kidding me?" said Clarisse.

Harry rested back in his chair, holding his cup of coffee in front of him. "Yes, Clarisse, he looked agitated. And, for someone who is a ghost hunter for a living, it made me feel kind of a weird."

"That may explain how you feel today," Clarisse said. She moved a little closer to Harry, sensing he was not himself. "Would you like some toast?"

"I don't have much of an appetite this morning; my stomach feels tense."

Clarisse put her arm around Harry's shoulders to comfort him. She understood the experience in the cemetery had rattled him and that it was unusual for a proclaimed skeptic to come to grips with it.

The growling sound of a modified Ford Falcon Ute echoed in the dining room as Paranormal Jack came screeching down the main street of Hartley. He skidded into the driveway of the presbytery, almost hitting the fence post that contained the signage.

Harry and Clarisse had a perfect view of the car park and the main street of Hartley from their table. The windows in the presbytery dining room that rose to the ceiling was typical of the grandiose architecture of the time. They did not make buildings like this anymore. The sunlight that streamed into the dining room through the satin curtains every morning created a warm ambience.

They both watched as Paranormal Jack briskly carried his recording device from the car and straight for the main entrance leading to the dining room.

Paranormal Jack knew his way around the place, and the townsfolk adored him as one of his own. And why not? He brought in the tourist trade and some well-needed cash into the community. Along with the weddings at Saint

Bernard's Church, his paranormal tours had become legendary with the city folk. For that, he got to share some of the spoils and the keys to the town

Paranormal Jack seemed to be in a hurry, particularly for a guy who liked to take his time. He rushed into the dining room, almost colliding with the waitress as he juggled his recording devices in one hand and his laptop in the other. He looked up to see where Harry and Clarisse were seated and nodded to signal his arrival.

"Hi, Harry and Clarisse. Can I put my stuff over here on the table next to you so I can lay things out?"

"That table is designed for six people, so there's plenty of room," Harry said.

Clarisse nodded, not saying anything.

"I got a chance to listen to the recording this morning and applied filter technology to get it clearer—"

"And what did you hear?" Harry was impatient.

There was a pause in Paranormal Jack's voice. For a jovial guy, he had become unusually introverted. "Do you want to know—"

"It's just curiosity value, Jack. I don't think we are going to take it all that seriously."

Jack squinted his eyes and creased his forehead. It was bothering him, and he didn't want to say it.

"I would like to hear it," Clarisse interjected.

"Okay. Don't say I didn't warn you." Paranormal Jack turned on his laptop and connected the recording device through a cable. He fiddled on his keypad and launched the program that would play the recording.

A screeching sound, like that of an animal in pain, filled the room, followed by static interference. Then, to the surprise of Harry and Clarisse, a deep, husky voice with baritone qualities and an old English accent.

*"One of you is going to die."*

The recording ceased for a few seconds, and then repeated. This time the static interference was more pronounced. The deep, husky voice changed to a joyful, female voice but with a local accent.

*"One of you is going to die. Ha-ha."*

Harry, Clarisse, and Paranormal Jack all looked at each other, silent and in disbelief. Then Clarisse reached out for Paranormal Jack's keyboard and pressed the pause button. She had heard enough and was concerned about Harry's reaction.

"What does this mean, Jack?" Clarisse asked, tense and emotional.

"You know, evil spirits and ghosts say things as a warning or omen." Jack put his head down and tightened his lips.

"In your experience, have you ever heard anything like

that before?" Harry asked.

"No." Paranormal Jack was despondent.

"So, are you taking it seriously, Jack?" Clarisse asked.

"I don't know what to think." Jack sat down on the chair next to Harry and took a cup, filling it with the remaining coffee in the plunger.

"What do you mean, you don't know? The recording said someone is going to die. Someone in this room?" Clarisse wanted answers and was not prepared to sit back and just accept it as a paranormal experience.

"This was a ghost town two years ago, and nobody came here. I had just started my paranormal tours," Jack reflected. "Maybe I upset the spirits. You know, always knocking on their door, so to speak. Maybe they've had enough of me ruffling their feathers. Perhaps I have pissed them off!"

"Maybe you have pissed them off, Jack." Harry crossed his arms and took a deep breath. "Do you believe there are evil spirits in the town?"

"Yes, I do. But these spirits are not troubled and unhappy; they are just manifestations of loneliness, not the sinister types. That's what makes the paranormal tours so successful. There is always a ghost or two that likes to show off during every tour."

"But nothing like this, right?" said Clarisse.

"No, nothing like this. I only experienced bagging doors, lights fading out intermittently, the occasional change in temperature, and weird sounds, but that's about it.'" Jack took another sip of his coffee to fray the nerves. "You remember the lights in the basement last night in the presbytery, Harry?"

"How could I forget?"

"That's not the first time that's happened. And there have been sightings of a ghost—Father Grimaldi—pointing toward the basement from his grave—"

"But never a threat like this?" Clarisse cut into the conversation. "Let me remind you what the recording said—someone is going to die."

Paranormal Jack reached out to take a muffin from the table. "I hope you don't mind. I gotta run."

"Is that it, Jack?" His sudden departure angered Clarisse. "You don't have a plan?"

Paranormal Jack seemed unfazed by Clarisse's reaction as he stood up from his chair and began to pack up his laptop.

"That's okay, Jack. I don't think Clarisse and I can eat them all. You can take more muffins for the road, if you like?" Harry said, trying to release the tension in the room.

"Just one for the road, then." Jack tried to balance his car keys, recording device, and muffins all in one hand like a circus juggler. "I will be back on Wednesday for my next paranormal tour."

"Well, why don't you come and see us before you start? As you can see, we will be the only ones in town."

"We start at seven p.m., as it's starting to get dark earlier now. It helps with the ambience. We can catch up before my tour starts." Paranormal Jack was struggling to carry his belongings, trying to maintain his balance by shifting side to side.

"It would be nice to have someone to talk to," said Harry. "I will see around six p.m., if that suits you? I can help you set up if you need a hand."

"I can always do with some help, Harry; that's for sure!" Paranormal Jack said from across the room.

Paranormal Jack made it to his car without dropping anything, but it took him twice as long as when he first arrived. He turned on his car, and the growling sound of the modified engine filled the dining room again. You always knew when Paranormal Jack was in town. He then accelerated onto main street at a high speed with his tires burning rubber with a screeching sound before he disappeared into the distance.

Harry and Clarisse looked at each other with a nervous grimace. A ghostly encounter with recorded evidence of a warning of something foreseeably unpleasant made her feel uncomfortable, like pins and needles and a sick stomach. She was concerned about the recording and the threat to Harry and Paranormal Jack by their ghostly encounter.

For Harry the Skeptic, there was a scientific reason for the recording—environmental factors, nature, or just a coincidence. Paranormal Jack was a local larrikin who just took it in stride. There was nothing he could not handle, preferring to brush it aside. As for Clarisse, it had sinister undertones. She preferred to explore further. Something was trying to warn them; frighten them away for a good reason. What was it?

It brought back memories of the superstition that manifested in her family for over a hundred years. Harry thought the superstition was fanciful and an old wives' tales, but he had never disrespected her culture. He understood that, to Clarisse and her family, superstition was deep-seated and rooted in their tradition.

Many would label her a spirit hunter or a spirit target. The world of the afterlife knew how to find her, a vestibule for spirits on the other side. It was an extraordinary power that she had inherited from childhood, and although she had not been aware of it at the time, people around her sensed she was different.

During her final days in her country, Clarisse had had to confront the superstition and succeeded. She had fought hard to remove the presence of the malicious evil and its influence from her family. She had put herself at risk from the maleficent that resided within, challenging its motives that it had garnished from the devil. It was the omnibus upon which the darkness influenced the lives of many in her community.

The next couple of days passed without any talk about the ghostly encounter. They both steered away from the topic and preferred to let it sit in the background.

Harry had been called out to the worksite, which was fifty miles outside of Hartley, to survey the new communication structure. He was due back in time to catch up with Paranormal Jack.

He liked Paranormal Jack, more so than he had at the beginning. The man sort of grew on you. His Aussie larrikinism, modified country-style Ute, and down-to-earth personality made Paranormal Jack fun to be around. It was what made his paranormal tours so successful.

He was a storyteller and knew how to narrate a spooky tale with all the ambience of the Hartley ghost town tag. Having grown up in the area and a descendant of the early settlers in Hartley gave him credibility. He was an authority in the field, its history, and its uneven past.

He knew more than what he let on. He had a trump

card in his pocket, and it was the real story of Hartley, which he kept under wraps, on a need-to-know basis, only giving you the snippets—the sinister side to Hartley.

Harry had a gut feeling that Paranormal Jack was not letting him in on Hartley's past and, only by getting to know him better, build a relationship, he could find out its history.

Although Harry was not as sensitive as Clarisse or in tune with the vibes of his surroundings—the energy, as Clarisse would put it—he sensed that the presbytery had an inconspicuous past. The church was beautiful on the outside, architecturally. On the inside, it beckoned a lack of ministry or a spiritual feeling. It showed in the monochrome pictures on the walls—solemn, anguish, sorrow, and a semblance of apathy in the eyes of the priests. They hadn't wanted to be here and were only carrying out orders from the Church—to obey and fulfill God's work at all costs, even in the most desolate and desperate of places.

Harry rushed back to Hartley, cognizant of his catch-up with Paranormal Jack before the commencement of the scheduled paranormal tour. As he drove into the main street and past the old police station and cells, a police car passed him in the opposite direction, heading out of town. Then an entourage of about twenty vehicles followed the police car. It was more traffic than Hartley would receive on a typical day.

Confused and unsure of what was going on, he stepped on the accelerator and skirted around the corner and into the presbytery driveway in a manner unusual for his calm self. He was too curious to find out what was going on. However, other than the cars exiting the town, he noticed there was no buzz in Hartley and Paranormal Jack's Ute was missing from the usual parking spot next to Saint Bernard's Church.

With a paranormal tour ready to start in thirty minutes, typically, the tourists would have started trickling in, and the souvenir shop across the road would be brimming with its lights on—it only opened on the paranormal tour days, and Paranormal Jack had a controlling stake in it, a profit-making venture in Hartley paraphernalia—but there was nothing.

Harry remained steadfast next to his car as he looked around, pointlessly waiting for the preshow to start.

Clarisse came running out of the Presbytery Inn, nearly losing her footing on the cobblestone steps that laced the entrance.

Harry turned toward her, instinctively knowing from her body language that something was wrong.

"Harry, I tried calling you! Why didn't you answer your

phone?" Clarisse was angry, grabbing ahold of him and squeezing his arm with all her strength.

"What's going on? Why are you mad?" Harry stood firm, not wanting to overreact. Something was not right.

"You mean, you don't know?"

"About what? I have been at work all day and the mobile phone reception is so bad out in the bush." Harry pulled out his phone to acknowledge all the missed calls and messages. They had loaded onto his phone as he'd arrived in Hartley with the better reception from the communication tower.

"He's dead!" Clarisse was sobbing.

"Who's dead?"

"Paranormal Jack. He died last night in the hospital. It was a car accident."

"What? Say that again ... He's dead?"

There was an inanimate silence as Harry clutched onto Clarisse and hugged her tightly. He was trembling and dropped his car keys and mobile phone where they crashed onto the pebble stone driveway.

"How did it happen?"

"He hit a tree driving home late at night. The police said he was trying to avoid something on the road," said Clarisse.

"An animal? There are lots of native animals in the

area." Harry took hold of Clarisse's shoulders and looked at her intensely.

"They don't know!" Clarisse continued hugging Harry, teary-eyed and sobbing. "The police just left as you arrived. They came to shut down the scheduled paranormal tour and …"

"And what?"

"They wanted to talk with you, Harry. They found the recording device in the boot with your name labelled on a USB stick."

"Well, I didn't do anything wrong." Harry looked at Clarisse, starry-eyed and with a stiff neck.

"No, no. The police were returning it. They thought it belonged to you, so I took it."

"Did you tell them about the recording. I mean, the premonition?" Harry asked.

"No, it didn't come to mind." She took a deep breath. "Should I have told them?"

Harry and Clarisse looked at each other intensely, as though a veil of evil had transcended into their lives. It was the recording that had worried Paranormal Jack. The premonition of death. But was it a coincidence? If not, was the message only meant for Paranormal Jack? Was there more to come in the pipeline of evil? Was the ghost of Father Grimaldi, the illusion of depraved souls, to be taken seriously?

For now, all they could do was console each other and not make too much of it. It was easy to concoct sinister theories that took on a mystical meaning to make sense of a shocking circumstance. That was the rational thinking of Harry. However, for Clarisse, this had taken on a different purpose.

She wanted to know more. Her curiosity in the supernatural meant she needed to explore the circumstances leading up to Paranormal Jack's death. There was the night in the cemetery and the voice recording, supposedly of Father Grimaldi, followed by a freaked-out Paranormal Jack who suddenly died in an unexpected car accident.

"Let's go for a walk to the church, Harry. I need to calm my nerves," Clarisse said, wanting to take solace in Saint Bernard's Church.

Harry took hold of her hand, gently at first, as they shuffled despondently along the pebble stone pavement, leaving a scuffed trail through the gravel in their wake.

To get to the church sooner, they decided to walk through the cemetery that held all of Hartley's past generations of residents who lay in silence with untold stories that they had taken to the grave.

Clarisse stopped at the marble gravestone that was much

taller than all the others. She read the inscription to Father O'Hara while removing an old flower pot with rotting flowers inside. It had been a while since the last person had placed flowers on his grave.

"Nobody looks after the graves here ... It's sad in a way," she said.

"I suppose all the relatives are long gone, and nobody cares anymore."

"Well, there are priests laying here; you would think the local municipality could spend money on its upkeep." Clarisse always felt that the Church had abandoned its flock in Hartley, considering they sent them thousands of miles to do God's work. Was this their just reward?

"It's such a shame that this whole cemetery was left derelict and uncared for. It's disrespectful," Harry said, nodding in agreement.

"It appears many priests died here. They are all lined up in a row," Harry said, spotting another marble gravestone.

As they stumbled around the tombstones and toward the entrance of the church, the ground underneath them was soft in parts from the evening rain. Weeds had taken over most of the gravesites, and some gravestones were leaning to one side, particularly those that had been hastily put together, laid in tradition but without the money for a proper burial.

Hartley had had its fair share of transients and vagabonds who had ended up in the cemetery alone and with no one to say goodbye to them. It had been left to the Catholic priests to attend to those lost souls and afford them a parting into God's kingdom. Whether they were believers or not, it made no difference. It was the missionary task to ensure Hartley was a Catholic town, bound by the traditions of the Church, and if it meant caring for lost souls and unbelievers, so be it.

Inside Saint Bernard's were brochures of the paranormal tour laid out in anticipation of the next tour by the caretaker. A signpost made of wood with the words, *"Paranormal tours this way,"* was a constant reminder that the next Paranormal Jack tour had been scheduled to kick off at this moment. It was a heavy feeling for Harry and Clarisse, as they sat in the last row of the beautifully preserved church.

Clarisse was silent and had something on her mind. She was not convinced about Harry's explanation about his evening in the cemetery. Something was missing. Call it a sixth sense or a feeling of spirituality; she was seeking clarity.

"Harry, did you tell me everything that happened that night with you and Jack?"

"Well…"

"I'm sensing there is more to the story, and you've only told me snippets of what you want me to hear."

Harry was silent, thinking some explanation might be required to save him from Clarisse's disappointment.

"I did not want to make a big deal of it—frighten you, I mean," he said. Harry's voice was choked and became hoarse.

"A big deal of what? You don't think I can take it?" Clarisse looked directly at Harry with her almond, fierce brown eyes locked in. It was not an intimidating look, but one of real concern of what they might have been getting themselves into since arriving in Hartley. "You should know me by now, Harry. I'm not scared of the dark side and the evil spirits that populate that sinister world. But I am concerned about that recording and the warning." Clarisse picked up the brochure in front of her and put it in Harry's lap. "He was supposed to be here right now, and he's gone, just like that."

"So, you think I'm next?"

There was a profound silence. Clarisse did not answer Harry's question but looked down.

"Well, is that what you think?" Harry reiterated.

Clarisse was still silent, trying to think of how to change the topic of conversation.

"So, what happened in the cemetery, Harry? If you can't

talk to me about it, then what type of relationship do we have?"

Harry looked embarrassed and red in the face. "Okay, Clarisse, here it is … I saw his face—Father Grimaldi. It was the face of the devil, and it frightened the shit out of me." Harry took a deep breath and positioned himself straight on the chair. "And yes, he pointed to both of us when we recorded the voice of evil." He looked straight at Clarisse, his eyes and forehead crinkling. "Are you happy now?"

"It was the devil's face?"

"Yes. Evil incarnate. The most horrible face I have ever seen."

"And what else, Harry? What else did you see?"

Although Clarisse was not a big person physically, petite at five-foot-three, she made up for it with her strong personality and conviction. It was one of the things Harry admired about her—her inner strength qualities.

"I saw flickering lights coming from the basement next to my office. And before you jump to any conclusions, Paranormal Jack said he had seen them before, a sort of electrical disturbance."

Clarisse sighed and crossed her arms, looking at Harry intently, not in an angry way, but pensive. Harry had seen this determined look before in Clarisse—almost investigative, like wanting to get to the bottom of everything.

"Do you think Paranormal Jack knew more than he was letting on?" she asked.

"It's something I thought about, Clarisse." Harry squinted.

"Well, you never know with people like that, the ones who have lived in the area for generations. There is always that little bit extra that they don't share with strangers."

"Now that I think about it, he was always giving extra snippets of information that people on his paranormal tours were not privy to." Harry clasped his hands and held them firmly at chest height, as it gave him comfort and confidence. "It was as though he was trying to whet my appetite, tap into my curiosity levels."

"Is that it, then? There is nothing more he told you?"

"Yes, that's it."

"And what about the lights in the basement? Do you have keys to those rooms?" Clarisse was digging deeper again and would not let go.

"The key I have only opens my office."

"I take it you have already tried to get into those rooms?" Clarisse turned toward Harry and adjusted her seating by crossing her slender legs and her arms across her chest.

Harry was silent, thinking about his next words. "I was curious … and I checked it out. Can't get into those rooms without the right key." Harry took a deep breath and looked to the side to avoid Clarisse's reaction. "I think you're assuming too much, Clarisse." Harry was starting to get annoyed with the line of questioning. Sometimes he felt interrogated by Clarisse when the issue piqued her interest.

"Oh, it's nothing. I'm sure it's like any basement room in an old house—full of junk and bits and pieces," Clarisse said.

"But something is bothering you; I can tell." Harry took her hand. "So, what is it?"

Clarisse did not want to raise past events, even though Harry was tenacious.

"Come on, Clarisse; out with it."

"It reminds me of the evil I encountered back home."

"I see, but that evil is gone. It's not following you around." Harry was his rational self again.

"It's not so much the evil spirit I'm thinking about, but the circumstances that are similar."

"What do you mean exactly?" Harry needed clarity and had difficulty trying to follow her perspective.

"I realized the evil that resided within was lonely, closed up in a solitary room without the opportunity to unleash its negative vices." Clarisse turned to the side on her seat.

"I concluded later on that it tried to lure people onto the chair, whether it was through smell or the scraping of moving furniture."

"Well, I remember experiencing the scraping of furniture from outside the room when I first visited your house."

"That's right, Harry. And I believe there is something in the basement trying to get us into the room."

"For what reason?" Harry asked.

"Who knows? To trick us, perhaps? Or to communicate from the other side?"

"You mean, it's a dark spirit, locked up inside?"

"Maybe I'm overthinking it. Could be an electrical problem with the lights in that room. It is a one-hundred-and-fifty-year-old structure; who knows how often the caretakers go down there?"

"Now you are starting to sound rational and as a skeptic." Harry pouted.

They had performed a one-hundred-and-eighty-degree about-face in their opinions—from the irrational to rational. It was Clarisse's way of diffusing any potential argument with Harry. She knew she had a testing personality when it came to the supernatural and unexplained events. It always pierced her desire to investigate unexplained phenomena—to get to the bottom of it.

There was the haunting of the ghost of Father Grimaldi, Harry's vision in the cemetery, the recordings presumably linked to Paranormal Jack's passing, and now the basement room. So, what lurked in those rooms, locked away and out of sight?

Harry left early the next morning to return to the communication site and continue his project work. He had to use his leadership skills to solve the problem and lead his team of technicians. He relished the opportunity to put his name on the successful completion of the project, on schedule and on budget. It would lead to other projects in the future and a rising career in his field. He would return later in the afternoon.

Clarisse was okay with being alone during his site visits. She could not say Harry didn't warn her of the possible boredom before accepting the role. It was either stay in Sydney and see him on weekends or enjoy the surroundings of a country town. However, having nothing to do provided her with the solace she craved—the opportunity to enjoy nature, to reflect on things and ponder. And even though Hartley was a ghost town between Monday to Thursday, excluding the mid-week paranormal tours, she always found something to do.

Clarisse was far away from her home, Manila, the City of Affection, and the twenty-four-hour hustle, her Southeast Asian culture that was full of vibrancy. She had grown up surrounded by the noise and lack of privacy—people at every corner, going about their business. So, for Clarisse, Hartley was a refuge, a touchpoint with nature and serenity that filled the soul.

As for Harry, he understood Clarisse's background, having spent much time in the City of Affection himself. He had struggled with the constant, in-your-face lifestyle of Manila, preferring the serenity of Hartley and the old English charm of its buildings and historic surroundings. In which case, it appeared to suit both for now for different reasons.

It was Friday morning, the day that wedding parties started arriving to prepare for the church ceremonies the next day. At one point, Clarisse was the only person having breakfast as she gazed out the window into the car park and main street of Hartley. She noticed there were more cars parked in front of the Presbytery Inn than usual. Then she watched the arrival of another couple in their vintage wedding car, a 1963 Rolls Royse Silver Cloud.

Couples started trickling into the dining room—two, then four, and then eight—the rising sound of chatter filling the air. Weddings always created a sense of vibrancy around the Presbytery Inn.

Clarisse sipped on her coffee in the hope that it would wake her up and keep her alert. She had not had a good night's sleep, thinking about the events of the day before. She was aware that overthinking was not good for her, mainly about things she had little control over.

Instinctively, she thought about the recording device and the USB stick that the police had left behind for Harry.

The police had always found Paranormal Jack a handful, and the local constabulary had known him for speeding on the main road outside of town. But they had also had a soft spot for him, having grown up together in the local district. They knew about his larrikin tendencies but also admired his entrepreneurship. He had been the one who had brought Hartley back to life, and later, he had come up with the idea of weddings in Saint Bernard's Church.

In an impulsive move, she decided to go back to her room and play the USB recording on her computer. As painful as it was, Clarisse wanted to hear it again, alone and without Harry, to see if they had missed anything significant. She had all the time in the world to go through the recording thoroughly time and time again.

Once in her room, Clarisse grabbed the USB stick with the identification tag still on it from the police. She expediently opened her laptop and plugged in the USB device. She was impatient, tapping on the desk with her right hand nervously, as it loaded up to the main screen. When it did, she grabbed the mouse with determined intent and clicked on the icon that would take her to the recording. Then she sat back in her chair and waited for it to load. It did not sound any better the second time—a husky and grizzly pitch that fluctuated in tone from high to low. It seemed like two people were speaking at once, an Irishman and a woman with a higher volume.

"*You are going to die. You are going to die,*" said the recording repeatedly.

It repeated the same phrase three times until a pause in the recording. It was the same pause that Harry and Clarisse had experienced the first time they had heard it. And then, as she was just about to rewind the tape, she captured another voice. It was a different person this time, with a deep tone and an accent that she did not recognize.

"*Utrumque, utrumque,*" the recording said.

Clarisse wrote the word down on her notepad, unsure whether she had spelled it correctly. She searched for its meaning on her home page, hoping to get a match. The internet at Hartley was rudimentary, and it relied on a slow wireless connection. It added to her frustration as Clarisse waited anxiously for the results to come in. Finally, after one minute, the reference to a Latin meaning scrolled across the screen.

*Utrumque - Latin for "both of you."*

Clarisse refreshed her computer screen then typed the word in again to confirm her findings, with a slightly different spelling. Still, the same result appeared on her screen.

*Utrumque - Latin for "both of you."*

She put the two phrases together to complete the sentence.

*You are going to die, both of you.*

Clarisse looked up, motionless and froze, as her face became numb. A tear formed at the left side of her eye then slid down her face.

The phantom that Paranormal Jack and Harry had encountered in the cemetery had pointed to both. She recalled Harry telling her the chilling story of how the infrared imaged had captured the ghost on the monitor screen, arms raised and looking toward them in defiance from its resting place.

Paranormal Jack was dead, and Harry was supposedly next in line. It could happen at any time; a freak accident at work or a car incident on the way home. Anything was possible.

Was it an omen, a curse, or a vendetta from a spiritually

unsettled ghost? The phantom was a cursed soul that had slid to the side of evil with its soul trapped in a relentless kaleidoscope of torments. Was this how it unleashed its pain and suffering? By making others pay the price?

Clarisse's instinct was to know more, to get ahead of the game and find out the basis for its evil curse. While most people would have run out of town, fearing the worse, to get away from the haunting as quickly as they could, Clarisse was smarter than that. You could physically run away from evil, but you could never hide. These metaphysical boundaries that we lived did not apply in the spiritual world where there were no impasses. A tempered evil spirit could follow you around from place to place forever. They could even occupy a physical state, like a piece of furniture or a doll.

Clarisse had to find a way of dealing with the evil without letting on to Harry.

Clarisse removed the USB device from her computer and placed it in her purse, a place that Harry would never look, respectful of her privacy. She also put the recording device in the bottom drawer, an empty drawer that Harry never used, as most of his essentials remained in his basement office. Clarisse was banking on Harry forgetting about the recording. He was busy at work, traveling between his office and the site. That left him very little time in the evening to think about anything else.

While Clarisse put away the recording device, she heard a knock on the door. It was a gentle knock at first, as though the person on the other side was trying to avoid the intrusion.

As she got up from her baroque armchair and walked toward the door, there was another sequence of knocks, quicker in succession this time.

"Hi, I am Eleanor, the caretaker ... I'm sorry to bother you, my dear. Is Harry around?" She was a frail, older woman, in her late seventies, carrying a walking stick.

"Hi, Eleanor, I'm Clarisse, and Harry's at work. He is onand-site today. Out in the bush, you know."

"Oh, what a nice accent you have, dear. Where is it from? It sounds American."

Clarisse smiled and blushed, unsure of how to deal with Eleanor's frankness. "I grew up in Manila, and it's American-English. We are taught it at school."

"Oh, what a beautiful city! I went there once with my late husband, George. He loved the culture and the people. He fought there during the war, you know, with the allies."

"Oh! It's always nice to meet someone who knows about my culture." Clarisse crossed her legs and leaned against the architrave, relaxed and enjoying the chat. "You know they call Manila the City of Affection?"

"I have heard that term before, my dear." She took a deep breath and pondered. "George used to say that many times—the City of Affection—now that I think about it."

"Yes, if you have spent time in Manila, you would have come across it, for sure. It's a term of endearment for the city."

"Oh, my dear, I did not want to hold you up, you know. I can talk for a long time once I get started."

"That's okay, Eleanor." Clarisse smiled. "I have all the time in the world. I'm not exactly fully occupied here in Hartley."

"Oh yes, good old Hartley town, off the beaten track and still practically a ghost town." Eleanor took out a mortice key and handed it to Clarisse. "Can you do me a favor, my dear?"

"Yes, of course, Eleanor."

"I'm out of town tomorrow, and I need someone to open up the basement for the delivery van." Eleanor's voice croaked as she spoke. "You remember Paranormal Jack?"

"Oh yes, we do." Clarisse had a real solemn look on her face as she looked down. "What a tragedy."

"God bless his soul. I have around twelve boxes of his possessions that we are going to store in the basement. He did not have any close relatives and lived alone, so I agreed to put away his stuff." Eleanor shook her head and smiled.

"Oh, he does have his grandmother, but she is in her eighties—we don't bother her with these issues. She lives in a nursing home not far from here."

"Well, that's very nice of you, Eleanor, helping out like that."

"I knew Jack's father and mother. They were lovely people. They lived on a farm just outside of town."

Clarisse took the key to the basement from Eleanor and placed it in her pocket. "No problem, Eleanor. I will be here to make sure the boxes are stored in the basement by the time you get back."

"Thank you so much, my dear. You're a real sweetheart." As Eleanor started walking away, she turned back before Clarisse could close the door. "Oh, and that basement ... you don't want to be in those rooms for too long. They are very creepy, and I avoid going down there." She looked at Clarisse intently and cringed. "I never feel right in those rooms. Even when I was a child, I hated that basement."

Clarisse waved goodbye to Eleanor then stood steadfast as she reflected on the older woman's passing comment. To some people, those words might have spooked them, but not Clarisse. She recalled Harry's recounting of the strange lights coming from there and how Paranormal Jack had seen it all before, too.

Clarisse's inquisitive mind meant she had access to the basement room and Paranormal Jack's possessions. It was an opportunity to learn more about the history of Hartley from an insider who had grown up in the area.

What else was she going to find in that library of information that Paranormal Jack had tucked away for so long?

Harry was going to spend all week at the remote site, managing the project. It would be a perfect time to inspect the contents of Paranormal Jack's belongings collected over the years. He had been the authority on the history of Hartley, and many travel magazines had interviewed him for his knowledge. They reveled in the mystique of a ghost town slowly coming to life by leveraging its unique landmarks and paranormal sightings. It made good reading for the magazines and helped bring the tourists back.

Who didn't like a good ghost story?

## 6 THE BASEMENT

Paranormal Jack's belongings had arrived, and it was more than the twelve cartons that Eleanor had indicated. It looked like the delivery people had thrown in some extra possessions, not knowing what to do with them. As for Clarisse, she did not know where to start. Luckily, Paranormal Jack was also an archivist and had labelled every box and its contents in detail. Every box had a comprehensive manifest, which helped Clarisse work through the materials.

She picked box number eight—family history—to start with and placed it on the antique console table just next to the stairs.

As she lay out the neatly organized files across the table, one caught her eye—Father Grimaldi. Inside were birthday cards, letters, and pictures of Father Grimaldi. One image that fascinated her was Father Grimaldi next the Paranormal Jack's grandmother, Louise. She had only been a child at the time, and they were standing outside Saint Bernard's Church. It was a charming black and white photo, typical of the time, with Father Grimaldi dressed in his black suit and white collar.

Clarisse turned the back of the picture to find a handwritten note.

> *To my dear niece, Louise,*
> *From Father Grimaldi.*
> *I'm so happy you're much better now, and*
> *God bless you always.*

Clarisse reread the note to make sure that Paranormal Jack was indeed related to Father Grimaldi through his grandmother. He had never let on to anyone about it. At least, that was what she thought. Perhaps this was what had driven him to be so entrenched in the folklore of Hartley. It was his descendants who had characterized the town and its cynical past.

Clarisse kept on looking through the box hastily until she found the hospital records of Father Grimaldi and his niece, Louise. They were the admission documents. It went into detail on the prognosis, their treatment, and recovery. How Paranormal Jack managed to get these records was incredible, because they were private information that belonged to the hospital.

Clarisse was anxious and impatient, wanting to go through every file sequentially and quickly, but it was not possible to sift through this treasure trove of information in a day. She would need to prioritize and become methodical to fulfill her desire to know everything about this ghost town and its tormented past.

Clarisse glanced over at another file. It was a police report and scrapbook, containing all the cuttings from the local newspaper and police investigation notes on the disappearance of Father Grimaldi.

A well-preserved clipping from the local paper caught her attention—April 1932 edition of the *Hartley Times*.

*The third priest in five years goes missing from Saint Bernard's Parish.*

There was another photo of Father Grimaldi standing next to the presbytery—a full spread of the front page of the local tabloid that had since become defunct.

*Search for Father Grimaldi finally called off after one week.*

Clarisse was intrigued, and her investigative personality was paying off by the discovery of long-held secrets that had almost disappeared with the ghost town tag. She was running out of time, however, as Harry was due back in an hour. The only thing she could do in the meantime was move the boxes to underneath the staircase, temporarily away from Harry's prying eyes, hoping that Harry would be working out of town again the next day.

Harry had fallen asleep, exhausted from his day trip out of town. Meanwhile, Clarisse was restless, tossing around in bed like an unsettled five-year-old. She had a lot on her mind, like an obsession that held her consciousness ransom. It was the archive boxes that kept her awake, a treasure trove of information that went back more than a century at her fingertips. All she had to do was go digging again into those dusty archives.

Starry-eyed, looking at the ceiling, she decided now was her moment.

Oh, and as for Harry, he slept like a log; nothing would wake him. He could sleep through raging thunderstorms and would not have a clue what was going on around him.

Clarisse put on her night robe and slippers before she started to slip out of the bedroom and straight for the door. As she passed the side table at the entrance of her room, she noticed Harry's flashlight, a tool of the trade that he used when investigating sites out of town. She was of two minds whether to take it, as it was eleven p.m. and the basement had no natural light. In the drawer underneath the flashlight were the keys to the basement room.

*Those keys might come in handy*, she thought.

The basement stairs were at the end of the long, winding hallway from her room. On the way, she would pass the black and white pictures in old-style golden frames on the wall. They were mostly crooked and dusty from over the years, but they told a story; the whispers of people long gone who had once graced this presbytery. There was always one photo that caught her eye most of all—a young boy of at least six years of age moping down at the camera with a desperate look of wanting to be found. It was inscribed on the bottom of the frame, "*In honor of Little Charlie, God bless your soul.*"

He was old enough to understand he was an orphan, seeking the desperate kiss of a mother and the caress of a father. It affected Clarisse each time to think this boy, who had grown up as an orphaned child and brought up by Irish priests residing in this presbytery, in what might have been the same empty rooms that lined the hallway.

Clarisse heard tiny footsteps and a giggle as she walked along the dimly lit corridor. The footsteps startled her, and she looked around. There was nobody there. She kept on walking for the basement door, but she was more attentive this time, on guard for anything unusual.

There was another run of tiny footsteps and a cheerful giggle of a child, probably a boy. She looked around again.

Nothing.

*What the hell is going on?* she thought.

Although Clarisse was calm and not frightened, it raised her senses. She was only two steps away from the basement door when she heard the running of footsteps again and a more cheerful giggle. She quickly turned the other way, and there he was, halfway down the hallway next to room number six.

It was a scruffy little boy with a moon face and ash-blond hair covering his ears. The brightest of blue eyes glowed in the dim light. He was wearing knee-length, grey shorts and a dirty-white, round collared shirt, buttoned to the neck. The knee-high socks and school shoes gave the appearance that he was in a school uniform. He was holding a rope with a noose at the end of it colored in dry blood. The boy was directing toward the basement door, encouraging Clarisse to go inside. It lasted for about thirty seconds, and then he faded away.

Clarisse stood stoic, heart racing and hands shaking, quickly frozen and immobilized at the thought that she had seen a ghost. Then she got herself together and realized she had seen that face before. And then it dawned on her.

*It's from the picture*, she thought.

She raced toward the picture on the wall and directed the flashlight to get an unobstructed view. It was Little

Charlie; she acknowledged the cunning resemblance. The ghost of Little Charlie was toying with her and asking for something. Maybe there was an object in the basement that Little Charlie wanted her to see?

Unperturbed by her latest experience, she walked back to the basement door. She turned the knob on the old oak door that still had the same mortice lock from one hundred and fifty years ago. It creaked and seemed to take forever. It was a chilling sound.

The basement was dark, so dark that she flicked on her flashlight to a high beam. She was looking for the light switch to the solitary ceiling lamp in the room. It hung from the ceiling and just above head height, probably hastily put together during the years when electricity was a discovery, as it looked of vintage style.

As she stepped down the staircase at a timid pace, it creaked and croaked with her every movement. She felt her grip underneath loosening with every step as each footstep negotiated a safe passageway through the unbalanced structure. The air was cold and uninviting, and it was so dark you could barely see one foot in front of you. The smell was stale of dampness and rotting wood. The air was unfiltered to the point you almost needed a mask to help you from choking.

She guided the flashlight around the basement as she

hung onto the keys with a taxing grip. She went straight to the archive boxes stored underneath the stairs. However, she stopped in her tracks when she heard the recognizable *click* of a lock coming undone. Then the door to one of the rooms in front of her moved slightly ajar.

She directed her flashlight directly at the entrance to see a gap. The door was not closed properly by the people who had delivered the boxes. At least, that was what Clarisse thought.

She had a decision to make as time was precious and not on her side: continue sifting through the archive boxes or explore the basement room that she now had access to. She thought about her next move, thinking aloud, her discerning mind jumping around like a trapeze act. Her adrenaline was starting to kick in, and the prospects of digging into the unknown stimulated her exploratory mind.

Clarisse shuffled her feet to the basement door and gently pushed it open with her index finger, cautious but not afraid. She turned her head around the side of the eighteenth-century oak design, gripping firmly onto the handle with just enough room to direct the flashlight into the room. Her gut was telling her there was something amiss, unnatural, a dark presence that occupied this dungeon.

It was a room lined with bluestone and an arch entrance. A stone pillar stood in the middle as a supporting foundation for the presbytery building, but it looked out of place.

The flashlight reflected from the spider webs in the ceilings as a silver lining.

*How could anything live here, let alone an insect,* she thought.

Lots of old stuff cluttered the back of the room, tossed around without no sense of organization. It was leftover possessions of the presbytery and the priests who had once resided here. Who knew what religious artifacts stood amongst the mess and the stories each one represented?

Behind all the clutter was a cobalt blue metal chest. Clarisse pointed the flashlight toward it, and it bounced back a blinding and pristine cobalt blue haze across the room. Clarisse did not know too much about trunks, yet this one looked like something from an old pirate ship, like in the movies. Unlike all the other stuff in the room, the casket was clean, polished, and in immaculate condition.

It pricked her inquiring mind. How could something so old look brand new in such a putrid place? It was odd, and something was not right about it. Like any paranormal element, it was meant to confuse and throw you off track. It was something Clarisse had experienced once before in her own country, amongst the superstition that had embodied her family traditions.

She waved the flashlight around the room once more, although more carefully this time to ensure she did not miss anything. The room felt morbid, and the only point of interest was the cobalt blue chest.

*What is inside the blue chest?* she thought.

She had another decision to make: go back to the archive boxes, continue working through Paranormal Jack's files, and complete her forensic study of Hartley, or continue exploring the room. Clarisse was unsure of what to do next.

"Oh, fuck this," she whispered. Clarisse turned around and directed the flashlight toward the basement door, ready to leave.

"Now, that's not a nice thing to say, my dear." It was a husky voice in the background that echoed from all corners of the room.

Clarisse stopped dead in her tracks and trembled, jolted by the unexpected voice that had an Irish accent.

"Who said that?"

"Oh, my dear, I am in this room, but you can't see me. I am here, there, everywhere. I can be wherever I want to be, anytime—in the past, current, or future."

"Who are you? You talk in riddles," Clarisse said.

"Don't bother with my articulate tongue—I am not from your time." The voice increased by another octave. "So, Clarisse, you didn't introduce yourself to me."

"You know my name?" Clarisse felt inquisitive about the presence in the room. Although she was of strong character, it did not stop her from feeling apprehensive. She developed a slight twitch to her left hand, and it extended to the flashlight, vibrating as she held it with a sold grip, clutching it to relieve the tension.

"I know everything about everything. It was the first gift given to me in return for agreeing to this desolate and damning life. The devil himself ordained me, my dear. I am his prodigal son; at his mercy as he consumes me with his laughter each day."

"The devil enjoys your suffering?'" Clarisse said intuitively.

"I am his enjoyment. He plays and toys with me, but I am not the only one. There are more like me scattered around the world."

"I don't quite understand …" Clarisse pointed the flashlight at the cobalt blue chest and held it there.

"Oh, you won't find me anywhere. In time, you will understand the darkness I come from and the life I live haplessly every day. The pain and suffering that I endure for the benefit of eternal existence, locked in chains to this horrid room of evil and dark souls. "

"You want me to feel sorry for an evil incarnate like yourself?"

"Ha-ha. Well said. You have a sharp tongue. I like that. But you are so naïve, my dear. You don't just leave a demon; you negotiate and give it something better than before, a prize, a gift from heaven."

"A clean spirit?" she said.

"You catch on quickly." His voice became tepid as it mellowed. "Yes, the cleaner the spirit, the stronger my case—my chances of leaving the devil incarnate."

"You have been searching for that clean spirit for a while?" Clarisse was testing the spirit at his own game, but she was careful not to intimidate him.

"Let's not talk about me. I am a boring topic. I would rather talk about you, Clarisse." The phantom was holding back. He was not in a hurry, as he had all the time in the world.

"I don't have much to say," Clarisse said. She was trying to avoid the conversation and not appease him.

"I know you have seen evil before. Touched it, smelled it, and defeated it. Well done, my dear! Evil entities like me don't often get beaten by mortals such as yourself."

"You know about that, too? About my family superstition?"

"Oh. Come on, Clarisse. Do not play dumb. I know about the evil that plagued your house for a hundred years."

Clarisse was silent and caught for words. She wanted to say something but couldn't.

"You don't need to say anything, my dear. The evil in the chair was an amateur and nothing compared to the powers I possess. It was happy to sit behind the cover of a chair for hundreds of years and occasionally destroy relationships for fun."

"Surely someone told you about this. You're trying to trick me," Clarisse said.

"We have our ranking system, too, a hierarchy. Beating that evil spirit was a fine job you did and a great way to start. That demon was an amateur and low on our pecking order, so don't get too excited about your achievement."

"I am leaving this room, dark spirit." Clarisse had had enough.

She tentatively made her way back to the basement door, not looking back.

"You will be back, my dear!"

Clarisse kept walking out of the room, focused on avoiding any further conversation.

"They all come back, begging for more. So will you," the phantom quipped.

Tiny little footsteps ran across the room, and a giggle of a child resonated from everywhere. She had heard that sound before—Little Charlie.

Clarisse looked back, and sitting on the cobalt blue chest was a little boy with ash-blond hair, holding onto his neck. He waved at her with an inviting smile.

She was startled at the sight of Little Charlie but not frightened of him. If anything, she felt sorry for this little rascal.

"Oh, don't worry about his neck marks, my dear. They can't hurt him anymore," said the phantom.

"What happened to him?"

"Ha-ha. Your priest, a man of God, did an excellent job on Little Charlie."

"I don't understand."

"You will. Archive box number five, out there underneath the stairs. You will find all the information you need."

Little Charlie giggled again while holding a rope that he swung around for fun.

Clarisse was not unnerved by the apparition of Little Charlie. He was a cheeky ghost living in a transient world where he had not passed to the other side. Why Little Charlie still occupied the grounds of the presbytery after all these years confused her.

"Why don't you let him go, phantom? He is only a little boy," Clarisse asked.

"Oh, my dear, I am not in control of Little Charlie. He won't leave this place. At least, not yet. He has a score to settle, and he's waiting for the right time."

The apparition of little Charlie disappeared, and the room became quiet again. Clarisse wanted more information, but the phantom had deliberately shut down the conversation and left.

As Clarisse dashed out of the room, the door slammed shut behind her with a thundering *clap*. It reverberated across the basement, lifting the dust from the floor and the staircase.

Clarisse jumped unexpectedly and dropped her flashlight onto the floor with the light directly in her face. Speckles of dust danced in the beams in a circular motion, creating a display of rhythmic dancing. She was dazzled and looked steadily at the light show before she snapped out of it. It was hypnotic at first as her eyes fixed on the dancing specs of dust particles, untouched for over a hundred years. Perhaps the phantom had put on a show for her as a parting gesture, or it had been pure coincidence.

Tired from the unexpected encounter with the phantom that had drained her mentally, she left the files for another day. She did take one piece of information left on top of an archive box. It was a photo of Father Grimaldi with his niece in front of Saint Bernard's. The other document was the medical records from the hospital. The two were so intertwined with each other—their illness, immediate recovery, and the disappearance of Father Grimaldi not long after. She wanted to continue the research to uncover more details.

From what had been a quiet and boring relocation to Hartley had turned one-hundred-and-eighty degrees. It had become a spiritual investigation into the dark corners of the ghost town.

Clarisse had a lot on her mind and no time to be bored—she was on a mission to get to the truth.

*I must not forget box number five*, she thought.

Clarisse was going to fess up to Harry about the boxes that had belonged to Paranormal Jack. He was so tied up with his work that he had forgotten about the Paranormal Jack saga. He was not thinking about it or asking questions, so Clarisse had chosen to leave it out of conversations. Irrespective, she was going to mention to Harry the evidence she had obtained about Father Grimaldi from the photographs and hospital records.

Why they remained in Paranormal Jack's possession for so long was a mystery. She knew Harry would try to connect all the dots methodically. It was all about the facts for him and not the spirituality.

Harry and Clarisse differed so much in their evaluation of the spiritual, bizarre, and unexplained phenomena. Clarisse tapped into her inner self-awareness, gut feeling, and sixth sense, while Harry played around with evidence—real data and logic. It might explain why he had tripped-out after his ordeal in the cemetery. Some events had occurred that he could not explain rationally.

Clarisse made her way out of the basement and back to her room, happy to be away from the dark, oxygen-deprived, dusty, lifeless environment that existed downstairs. It was a different world.

*I better return the keys to Eleanor,* she thought.

Clarisse recalled she did not lock the door to the basement room. Caught up in her eagerness to get out swiftly, she had left it unlocked.

Eleanor had also returned from her day out of town to resume her caretaking duties. However, things moved slowly in Hartley, and Eleanor was not pressing to get the keys back. Hadn't even had a thought whether Paranormal Jack's belongings had been delivered. Clarisse assumed Eleanor would ask in due course and get around to it, eventually. No rush.

Harry arrived from the remote site, all happy that they

had resolved a major stumbling block with the communication tower. It was a project glitch that had gone wrong for several days until Harry found the problem. In the end, it had been a simple fix and not a significant concern.

He didn't waste any time. He was hungry, so he went straight for dinner. There was only one other couple in the dining room. They were an early arrival for a wedding scheduled the next day. The couple had come in before the bridal party to explore Hartley in more detail and catch the paranormal tour, not realizing Paranormal Jack had died. It was frequently an occurrence as random visitors drove into town, hoping to get on the tour, impromptu with no booking.

Clarisse waited for the right time to unleash onto Harry about the archive boxes in the basement. She had worked out that the best time to discuss controversial subjects was after his dinner, when his stomach was full and he was relaxed.

"Harry, I want to tell you something interesting I found," Clarisse said.

"Knowing you, Clarisse, I bet it's got a lot of mystique around it, so I am looking forward to it." Harry laughed.

"Don't be silly. You're going to find this interesting, if you can keep an open mind and not be so skeptical."

"Okay, tell me. What have you found?" His eyes were fixated on her.

"I'm not sure if you have noticed the boxes stacked in the basement, just underneath the stairs?"

"Oh yeah, I saw those yesterday. I thought they were using it as a storage room, Made nothing of it."

Clarisse pulled back her hair and fiddled with it, a nervous reaction. "They belonged to Paranormal Jack."

Harry stood silent and raised his head with eyes wide open, expressionless and stoic. "You're kidding me?"

"No, Harry, I'm serious."

"And I suppose you have already peeked at the boxes; found something of interest?" Harry was onto it. He knew Clarisse's curiosity would get the better of her.

"I did find something and thought of showing you. Have a look at these photos." Clarisse handed over the picture of Father Grimaldi standing next to his niece. "Do you recognize the building in the background?"

"Yeah, it's the church ... and that building next to it is where we are right now—the presbytery."

"You have a good eye for detail, Harry." Clarisse smiled. "Have a read of these documents."

"What—hospital records?" Harry clasped the documents tightly.

"Yes, records of when Father Grimaldi and his niece

were in the hospital for an undiagnosable illness." Clarisse pointed to the doctor's comments at the bottom. "Read these comments below, Harry."

Harry took his time as he sat back in his chair, deciphering the nineteenth-century handwriting. "They used to write very nicely in those days. *1936, Doctor Jamieson, head of the ward for infectious disease.*"

"Have you read it?" Clarisse asked impatiently.

"Yes, the doctor did not expect them to survive the illness, and then goes on to say they found the cure during a routine blood test they had missed altogether—pure chance."

"It was as if someone told them to look at the blood test again; led them in that direction."

"That's your opinion, Clarisse, but it doesn't say that, does it?" Harry said. He was always pressing on Clarisse to show the facts.

"Well, how else did they find the cure for their condition? They missed the diagnosis in the first blood test. When a second pathologist reviewed it, they found what was causing their bodies to shut down, and just in time, according to his notes."

"Oh yes, I can see that in the notes below. It says that they don't normally review the blood test the second time," Harry replied.

"Yes, and the person who reviewed the blood test the second time didn't know about the blood samples they had been previously analyzed."

Harry lifted himself from the chair to grab a second round of coffee from the plunger and handed back the notes to Clarisse. "It's a weird set of circumstances, even for a skeptic like me, or ..."

"Or what, Harry?"

"Maybe a coincidence ..."

They both looked at each other, waiting for the first person to react. Clarisse and Harry had hit an impasse, which usually happened when trying to decipher unexplained events.

While Harry buttered his bread roll, he asked Clarisse an impromptu question. "There is something you're not telling me, Clarisse, and I can see it in your face. Come on, out with it."

Clarisse did not overreact as she took a mouthful of rice, preferring to take her time. "Father Grimaldi's niece is the grandmother of Paranormal Jack."

Harry froze. "You're kidding me! He's related to Father Grimaldi? The same ghost he follows during his paranormal tours?"

"Yes ... and I have more news for you."

"You mean, there's more?" Harry was intrigued.

"I have found out that Paranormal Jack's grandmother is still alive, in her late-eighties, at a nursing home twenty miles out of town."

Harry and Clarisse remained silent, knowing what each other were thinking instinctively.

"How on earth did you find that out?" Harry asked.

"Eleanor, the caretaker, when she asked me to make sure the boxes were properly stored." Clarisse had a sparkle in her eyes. It was the type of expression when she was onto something, and Harry had seen it before.

"Should we go for a drive tomorrow and meet her? What's her name?" asked Harry.

"Louise Grimaldi. The aged care facility is on the road to the next town."

"I had a feeling you already looked it up, Clarisse." Harry laughed.

"Ha-ha. Of course. I have all the time of the world in Hartley."

"Yes, Hartley is perfect for an investigative mind. I find it useful myself when I'm working on complex work problems." Harry handed back Clarisse the photos. "So, what do we tell Louise? Why are we visiting her?"

Clarisse smirked and said, "Tell her we are writing a story on Hartley and her name came up in the archives. We are talking to several people, right?"

Harry reclined back in his chair and stretched his arms before placing them on his head, saying, "I can live with that as an explanation. It's a half-lie."

"You mean a white lie, Harry?"

"Yeah, a white lie."

Clarisse did not tell Harry about Little Charlie. It would have been too much information for him in one sitting. She did end up scrummaging through the archive box number five, finding evidence about the boy's demise.

Inside the archive, the box was a confidential police report from Detective Hickes and pictures of the dig site of the grave. One picture was so gruesome that she could not bear looking at it again. Little Charlie was laying on the ground with a blood-stained rope next to him. She knew how he had met his fate—he had been hanged under cruel circumstances.

She wanted Harry to read the police report. With his analytical mind, it would have been a perfect task for him, and Harry would have liked chunk-sizing it down into factual points.

Detective Hickes had concluded with more than one theory, but there was one that stood out most. It had to do with his suspicion of two priests from the presbytery, although the case was never solved and file closed ten years after Little Charlie's death. It was an intriguing cold case and one that had more questions than answers. Clarisse promised herself that she would talk to Harry about it on their way to see Louise Grimaldi at the aged care facility outside of town.

# 7 THE CANDIDATURE

The drive to Fairhaven Aged Care Center was pleasant as they passed by many farms on the crest of undulating green hills. It had a typical Australian countryside smell—gum trees, eucalyptus, and shrubs amongst the tall grass. Cows in their abundance grazed on the grass growing in the fertile soil, and livestock roamed the corners of each farm. As the sunlight filtered through the sunroof of Harry's Ute, it kicked in the endorphins that accentuated the scenic trip. They were both happy to be out of Hartley and doing something different together for a while.

"Harry, I forgot to mention something …"

"Yeah, what was it?" Harry interrupted.

"I found something interesting while going through Paranormal Jack's boxes in the basement." It was an impromptu comment while she sipped on her traveling coffee mug.

He turned his head while driving with one hand at the

wheel. "Sure, what did you find? I bet it's interesting, hey?"

"I think you will find this very perplexing." She looked at Harry and smiled.

"Come on; tell me. Now you have me intrigued."

"Okay. I discovered this in archive box number five. In 1936, a six-year-old boy went missing from the orphanage, and after months of searching, they found no trace of him." Clarisse took another sip of her coffee. "Want me to continue?"

"Oh yeah, I recall Paranormal Jack mentioning his disappearance. It's starting to sound interesting."

"His name was 'Little Charlie,' and after eight months of no further investigation, a local detective by the name John Hickes was given a tip-off by a note that he received in the mail."

"Oh, a single note just magically appeared. I like those stories. And did they find the boy?" Harry was a little sarcastic and testy with Clarisse.

"Yes, they dug a hole next to the pond behind the orphanage and found him in a shallow grave." Clarisse was quiet as she gathered her thoughts. "I have pictures from the police file of Little Charlie before and after he died. Very gruesome, and it brings tears to your eyes."

"You looked at the photos of a dead little boy?"

"Yes, Harry."

"Do they know who did it?"

"Well, I have the police report on the investigation, and I was hoping you could help me—"

"Help you go through it?" Harry interrupted.

"Yes. You have a detailed mind for facts. You would be the best person to appraise it." Clarisse grinned at Harry, almost sarcastically.

"You mean I am the perfect skeptic?"

"Well, something like that."

"Sure, Clarisse. I will go through the police report tonight. Who knows what I will find? Probably nothing."

"Now you're jumping to conclusions, Harry."

"Yeah, I guess I should not prejudice the findings." Harry pulled down his window halfway to let the fresh country air into the car. With his hair blowing frantically in the wind, he looked at Clarisse with a churlish grin. "I might find a ghost did it."

Clarisse smirked and placed the file on his lap. "There you go. I will be interested in your opinion tonight."

Harry nodded and kept on driving with one hand while the other held the file. They were only a couple of miles out from the Fairhaven Aged Care Center.

He liked to be a sleuth and get his teeth into controversial bits of information, just like he did with Paranormal Jack—look for cracks in their beliefs and prove people wrong. He was the perfect skeptic.

Fairhaven Aged Care Center specialized in looking after the elderly who were becoming senile. They were losing their memory and thoughts of others that had been close to them throughout their lives. To what extent Louise Grimaldi was affected was unknown, so they had to play it by ear.

Fairhaven promoted the visiting of their residents to families and encouraged volunteers to spend time with the elderly. Getting through the front desk to see Louise would be a simple task of having the right script—they were writing a news article on Hartley and wanted to get a perspective on life in the earlier days.

Harry parked the car in the gravel car park next to the visitor's entrance. The facility looked like a throwback from the eighties and a place caught in time. It was off the beaten track and in the middle of nowhere. Nobody cared about its appearance architecturally as long as they provided the right care for the elderly.

They made their way to the entrance and walked into a reception area with tones of retro interior decorating from the eighties. It was a shabby chic look with lots of plants and an unframed wall mirror. The curtains were lined with striped pastel colors, and the carpet was dark green. A glass coffee table adorned the waiting area with useless magazines that were out of date and nobody read anymore.

"Hi, how can I help you?" the nurse at reception asked.

"We are here to visit Louise Grimaldi. We don't have an appointment and wanted to surprise her. Is she available?" Harry was sticking to the script that he had agreed to with Clarisse.

"Oh, isn't that nice? She does not get many visitors, the poor woman." The nurse pulled out the visitor's logbook and flipped it over several pages until she found Louise Grimaldi. "Wow, the last visit she had was Jack, six months ago. I'm sure she would welcome someone to talk to."

"Is she lonely?" Clarisse asked.

"I know her quite well, and she never complains much. She has no family, except Jack, who was her grandson, if I recall."

"Oh yes, Jack. That's Paranormal Jack. We did catch up with him on several occasions and went on his paranormal tour," Harry said.

Clarisse nudged Harry in the leg with her knee so he would keep his mouth shut. He was overtalking the introduction, and it was not in the script.

The nurse placed the sign-in book in front of Harry and said, "Can you both sign here, and then I will take you through to the alfresco area. That's where she likes to be at this time of day. A woman of routine, you know."

"Oh, it's a nice, sunny day, so that would be the perfect place to meet her," Harry said.

"And what exactly do you do again?" The nurse was curious. "I am supposed to ask everyone who walks into this facility. Procedures, you know."

"Oh, that's not a bother. We understand you doing your job." Harry smiled and pulled out his notepad. "We are writing a historical piece on Hartley, and we heard that Louise is a long-term resident of the town. That is, she has recollections of what the town was like before it became a ghost town."

"Yeah, good old Hartley. She always babbles on about the town and what life was like when she was a young girl." The nurse looked directly at Harry and Clarisse and put her hand over her mouth, whispering, "By the way, she is getting senile and may think you're her grandson, Jack. She even calls our visiting doctor Jack. Other than that, her recollections are sharp for a woman of her age."

"Thanks for letting us know. If she thinks I am Jack, I will just go along with it," Harry said.

"Yeah, that's what the doctor does—goes along with it." The nurse pointed the way to the alfresco area. "One other thing I forgot to mention …"

"Yes?"

"She may babble on about this boy. She calls him Little Charlie." The nurse looked directly at Harry and Clarisse with a cheeky grin and whispered, "I think she has created this person to keep her mind busy."

"Oh, I see." Harry smirked and nodded. "I'm sure we can work around that one, also."

The nurse escorted them through the narrow hallway. It resembled a retro eighties time tunnel tour with plants lining the walls every ten feet on pine plant holders. The walls were pastel pink wallpaper that blended with the dark green carpet and abstract art on the wall. The vintage picture frames appeared out of place in today's modern decor. At the end of the hallway was a double glass door with plantation shutters on either side to the alfresco area.

Louise Grimaldi was in her wheelchair, having lost the capacity to walk on her own, facing the garden. She was doing nothing and appeared to be daydreaming.

Harry and Clarisse introduced themselves as writers doing a piece on Hartley for a travel magazine. They all sat together in a lovely Tuscan garden that was geometrically designed with garden hedges and lavender. The comfortable garden furniture and layout of the garden provided an Italianesque feel.

"Hello, Jack. It's great to see you again, my dear," Louise said.

Clarisse nodded and whispered to Harry, "Just go along with it."

Harry nodded in acknowledgement. "I am good, Grandma, and it's great to see you again."

"So, who is that lovely girl with you, Jack? She is beautiful. Too good for you, I must say."

"I'm Clarisse, Miss Louise, and pleased to meet you."

"Oh, what a lovely accent you have, my dear. Is that American?"

"No, we call it American-English. I'm from the Philippines."

"Oh yes, the Philippines. My friend Eleanor, at the presbytery in Hartley, always talks about your country. I think they have visited the Philippines many times."

"Grandma, Clarisse is writing a story on the history of Hartley and would like to ask you some questions about Father Grimaldi," Harry asked politely.

"So, what prompted you to want to write about Father Grimaldi?" Louise queried.

Clarisse was caught off guard and needed to think quickly. "Well, Louise ... apparently, it became really popular with the paranormal tours ... but we didn't just want Paranormal Jack's explanation. I thought you could provide some real history on his mystery."

"You want to talk about my uncle, the now-legendary

Father Grimaldi, famous for all the wrong reasons? He went missing after we both left the hospital." Louise adjusted her posture on the chair. "My dear, I was lucky to survive."

"Can you tell Clarisse more about him, Grandma?" Harry asked, trying to keep her from wandering off.

"Can you pass me that glass of iced tea, my dear?" Louise asked. She sat back in her chair and sipped on the long glass. "Nothing like an ice-cold tea on a day like today."

"About Father Grimaldi, Grandma …"

"Oh yes, sorry, my dear. My memory is not like it used to be." Louise took a deep breath and placed the iced tea on the side table next to her. "They say he went missing, but that's not true. He still hangs around that house in Hartley."

"You mean the presbytery?" Clarisse said.

"Oh yes, I can't remember words as I used to."

"That's okay, Grandma. I am forgetful, also." Harry smiled. "Now, about Father Grimaldi, do you mean he still hangs around because of the paranormal stuff that's been happening?"

"He's not a ghost in the way we think. He lives in another reality, a spirit world that he cannot leave." Louise peered right into Harry's eyes to make a point. "I know because I had conversations with him many times when I was growing up."

"You have spoken to him?" Harry was blindsided and had not expected this level of frankness.

"You probably think I'm mad like everyone else." Louise stopped dead in her tracks and went silent.

Harry poured a glass of water from the jug and handed it over to Clarisse before filling his own. "It's okay, Grandma. We are not here to judge you," Harry said.

"He saved my life when I was in the hospital. He paid a hefty price and suffered a life of slavery to that demon." Louise was beginning to look teary as she looked down and wiped her eyes with her handkerchief.

"He told you that himself?" Clarisse was starting to blend into the conversation.

"Yes, my dear, and everyone thought I was hallucinating when I told the story. I was only a teenager when I first gathered the courage to confront him at the presbytery."

Harry and Clarisse became silent, and a sense of numbness penetrated their bodies from head to toe. Harry was unsure where to take the conversation and looked to Clarisse for help, his eyes inviting her to take over. It was the gaze of a man who could not absorb the supernatural elements. He was a skeptic, preferring that someone more in tune with the spirit world lead the questions.

"So, what is it with all the silence?" Louise said. She pointed to the teapot and the puffed pastries on the table in front of them. "Let's have some tea and pastries."

They filled their cups with tea and helped themselves to the pastries.

"They are made in the local bakery with all the natural ingredients you would expect from the local farming community," Louise explained.

Harry couldn't stop eating them and helped himself to more without any feeling of embarrassment.

"The pastries are delicious, Grandma!" Harry said while munching on a mouthful.

"I wanted to ask you how Eleanor is doing now that she has more customers staying at the presbytery?" Louise asked.

"I just met her for the first time a couple of days ago, and she is a lovely lady. Keeps herself busy by the looks of things. I don't see her around much," Clarisse said. She was trying to join in the conversation again the best way she could.

A small breeze blew across the table, almost dislodging the napkins and lifting the classic white tablecloth. With it came a beautiful fragrance of flowers, something that Clarisse had smelt before in her home country.

"It smells like Sampaguita," Clarisse said while looking

directly at Harry.

"What is that word, my dear? Sampa … sampa … Oh, I can't pronounce it," Louise asked.

"It's what we call a white jasmine flower in my country, and it's the sweetest smell. It's so similar it brings back memories," Clarisse said.

"Of course, my dear. We have lots of jasmine in our garden, and you have a perfect sense of smell for flowers. I'm very impressed," Louise said with a soft smile.

"Thank you, Louise. I can see some white jasmine over there nestled between the hedges."

Louise looked toward the white jasmine and acknowledged them, perfectly placed between box hedges and a paved pathway.

"You know why they call Eleanor *'the candidature'*?" Louise asked in a deliberate attempt to shift the conversation.

"No, we don't," said Harry.

Louise leaned forward and dropped her tone. "There have only been two candidates since the beginning of Hartley. She is the remaining one entrusted to do that job."

"We don't know what you mean, Grandma?" Harry was amiss with her point of view.

"Oh, yes, my dears. Her job is a double-edge sword. She sources potential candidates for Father Grimaldi. She does this to please him, and by doing so, he stays clear of the presbytery and church altogether. It's like an arrangement that's been in place for over eighty-four years."

"I'm sorry, Grandma, what type of candidates are you referring to?" Harry responded.

"There is only one way my uncle can leave his dreaded and insane existence." Louise stared glassy eyed into the vastness of the garden. "He needs to find a replacement. And not any type of replacement; one who would appeal to his master—the devil."

"You would never think she is the candidature," Harry said in disbelief.

"Ha-ha. You need to get over her gentle and fragile demeanor. That's the façade she uses to draw you into her charm. A Venus fly trap for unsuspecting people like yourself."

Clarisse and Harry were speechless and astonished. Should they believe this woman who fluctuated on the edges of senility? Was she delusional about a candidature that doubled-up as the human conduit for the phantom?

"You probably think I'm a senile old woman," Louise said, sensing that her visitors were not buying into her tales.

"It's not that we don't believe you, Grandma. We met Eleanor, and we could not imagine her canvassing for the phantom in such a way," Harry said.

The conversation with Louise was becoming difficult. Harry signaled to Clarisse that it might be time to say goodbye.

"I think we need to get going, Grandma, before sunset. You know the roads are not the best around here," Harry said.

"Oh, I understand, my dears. They haven't fixed those roads for over thirty years; potholes everywhere and neglected." Louise smiled and placed her teacup on the side table next to her. "Say hello to my Little Charlie when you see him next. Gorgeous boy, always giggling and full of life."

Clarisse and Harry stood still in their tracks and looked at each other.

"Not now. We will talk about it in the car," Clarisse whispered. She held onto Harry's arm, encouraging him forward to the exit.

Harry nodded and did not continue the conversation with Louise.

It was difficult trying to have a rational conversation with an absentminded woman. Even more problematic was trying to determine what was fact or fiction, or somewhere in between.

They said their goodbyes, hugged Louise, and thanked her before making a swift exit to the car as they whisked past reception, waving goodbye to the administrator.

Clarisse and Harry looked at each other and did not say a word. The ride back home was going to be long and drawn out. They questioned if they got more than they had bargained for and whether the encounter with Louise threw fuel into the fire.

Clarisse felt tingles in her stomach, and she clutched her abdomen to relieve the tension. She had not come clean with Harry about her encounter with the very person whom Louise had mentioned—Little Charlie. And the sense of guilt deprived her of the ability to hold a rational discussion about *the candidature.*

She had met Eleanor at the presbytery, and she was exactly how Louise had described her—inviting, sweet, and comfortable to chat with. Clarisse was drawn to her politeness and hometown hospitality—eager to help whichever way she could. But was she being conned? Set up for another encounter with the phantom to satisfy his pleasure?

For the time being, all she could do was open her window and smell the air. She cherished the Australian countryside and the gum trees that they passed on the main road to Hartley. It was a pleasant smell—natural, clean, and synonymous of the landscape. She could spend all day outdoors and soak it in, inhaling through her nostrils with deep breaths. For Clarisse, it was nature's gift, and she cherished every minute of it.

As for Harry, all he could think about was thrusting the accelerator of his Ute and making it growl. He loved driving on the straight country road and navigating through the hillside curbs to test his driving prowess and occasionally turn his head to see if Clarisse was impressed with his ambitious foray. Clarisse would smile in acknowledgement to make him feel good without saying anything, offering no opinion.

Clarisse and Harry drove into main street Hartley as the sun started setting over the gum trees in the distance. They drove by the old police station and cells that were once part of the Paranormal Jack tour. A warm breeze caressed their faces, and the sunset lined the clouds with a red-orange tinge.

Harry placed his eyes over his ten-dollar gas station sunglasses to restrict the intense glare. It was Sunday, and the only welcome sign was a derelict signpost battered with rogue gunshot holes.

Harry had enjoyed his day out, driving around the countryside and pushing the pedal on his Ute. It had provided him with a sense of freedom.

As soon as they arrived at the presbytery, he made his way to the dining room to grab a pot of coffee and to read the file on Little Charlie. Louise Grimaldi had piqued his interest. Plus, an original police file and a cold case that was unsolved from over eighty years ago. It was better than a detective movie, and he got right into it.

Clarisse, on the other hand, wanted to settle her nerves and stroll alongside the pond adjacent to the presbytery. She only had thirty minutes of sunlight before it became pitch black, enough time for her to walk around the pond once and get back before the natural light faded.

The tall eucalyptus tree mentioned in the police report was directly in front of her. It stood like a beacon, overseeing the entire garden, a distinctive landmark. She walked briskly toward it, knowing this was the location where Little Charlie had met his fate and where Detective Hickes had discovered his body.

As the crisp breeze caressed upon her back, the sound of the eucalyptus leaves swayed in the wind. The last rays of sunshine that filtered through the branches made her feel sublime. It was an eerie thought to think that, one foot in front of her, a little boy, no more than six years old, had been lain to rest unceremoniously.

Clarisse looked around, almost waiting for something to happen. The encounter with Louise Grimaldi had her wired up and made her sensitive.

Next to the eucalyptus tree was a small plaque made of

marble that almost went unnoticed. Clarisse moved closer to get a fix on the inscription.

*In memory of Little Charlie*
*May he rest in peace*
*Lithgow Police*

Clarisse had read in the police report how the constabulary had been affected by his gruesome find. It had left a legacy on the gravediggers, and particularly on Detective Hickes.

The sunset was making way to night, and the light around her was becoming dim. The shadows of gum trees that lay across the pond paled as the water in the pond became darker. The only source of light was from the lampposts in front of the presbytery car park. It was time for Clarisse to leave the lake and walk back to the presbytery. She was leaving behind that gut-wrenching feeling of Little Charlie's first resting place.

Making her way back again, she heard the giggle of a little boy echo amongst the shrubs. She was not frightened, knowing it was Little Charlie. Next came the footsteps of a child running between the fauna, stepping on loose leaves and tall weeds. There were more giggles and another series of footsteps, a little closer this time. Then it all went quiet.

Clarisse stopped in her tracks, halfway to the presbytery. "I know it's you, Little Charlie," she called out.

There was no response to her call.

"I know all about you, Little Charlie. I know what they did to you. Those bastards!"

There was still nothing, and a dead silence descended on the pond. Even the night animals did not make a sound.

She felt something was not right and started pacing back toward the presbytery. Clarisse had trouble navigating her way through the path, as she could not see in front of her very well and struggled to maintain her footing.

*I'm nearly there*, she thought.

She could see the light filtering from the lamppost through the shrubs, only twenty feet away.

Clarisse jumped. Something had bit her ankle. She stopped momentarily and turned to see the face of Little Charlie staring at her with his ash-blond hair, red eyes, and a sly grimace.

He was not giggling but growling and holding his hands in a scratching motion above his shoulders like a feral cat.

"Little Charlie, why did you bite me?" Clarisse said. She lifted her right ankle and inspected the wound. Blood trickled from the bite, and Clarisse was in pain.

There was another growl from Little Charlie, and she looked up. He was next to the shrub with his hands around his neck marks, moving them in a caressing motion, and then he disappeared.

"Come back. I can help you!" Clarisse yelled across the shrub. Her voice echoed in the distance.

There was a dead silence. It was pitch black with only the filtered light of the lamppost reflecting off the leaves of lilly pilly shrubs to help her focus.

Little Charlie was gone.

Clarisse realized this cute little boy had a sinister side to him, and he was not as innocent as his looks portrayed. She pondered how his murder affected his soul and how the evil phantom in the basement had influenced him. Little Charlie might have become the servant of the devil in the basement, just like Eleanor was his candidature. Their roles were to draw people to the basement for assessment by the phantom, to see if they were qualified as the perfect replacement, enough to satisfy the prerequisites of his master, the devil.

Clarisse made it to the steps of the presbytery, where Harry was patiently waiting for her. He was seated at the outdoor table on the porch, reading the police report on Little Charlie.

"I was waiting for you, Clarisse. What took you so long?" Harry was concerned that she had overstayed her walk around the pond. "I was just ready to come and look for you."

"Oh, I lost track of time. I found a plaque in memory

of Little Charlie next to the eucalyptus tree, believe it or not, and I got sidetracked."

"You mean the boy in the police report?" Harry asked. Then he looked toward her ankle and saw the bloodstained skin. "What happened to your ankle?"

"It was getting dark, and I could not see very well … I stumbled on a pothole and hit a large stone."

"We should get that bandaged before we have dinner," Harry said.

"It's nothing, just a scratch, and I have put a tissue on it." Clarisse thrusted her leg toward Harry to show him the wound. "See? It's nothing."

Harry held her lower leg to have a closer look. "It looks like a bite. Did something bite you? A snake?"

"No, it was not a snake. It just looks that way." Clarisse pulled down her leg and put pressure on her scratch with the tissue. "See? It's stopped bleeding already. It's nothing."

"You look like you've seen a ghost. Are you sure you're all right?" Harry was concerned about her white complexion and wide-open eyes. She did not look well.

"I'm fine, Harry. Just tired. Been a long day."

"Yeah. Besides the nice drive out of town, there's been too much information to soak in." Harry pulled out a chair and asked Clarisse to sit down. "I have read the police report."

"And did your skeptic mind find anything interesting?"

Harry shifted in the chair and took hold of the police report, shuffling the pages until he found the key section. "Look here. This part is interesting. I think Detective Hickes was aware of who committed the murder."

"Show me," said Clarisse.

"He states one of the Irish priests who died six months later was responsible. But because of his death, he could not prove it."

"What about the other priests, and Father O'Hara who was in charge?"

"That's a good question, Clarisse. From what I can gather, they were all tight-lipped about it, and Detective Hickes could not get anyone to provide evidence."

"So, the investigation went nowhere?"

"Correct. Round and round in circles until they closed the case."

They both remained silent and did not say anything for a while. It was uncanny for either Clarisse or Harry not to mention a word.

"What is it called when the priests won't reveal another person's confession?" Harry asked.

"I think it is called the sacramental seal." Clarisse paused for a moment. "I think I know where you are going with this."

Harry smiled. "Yeah, if the priest who murdered Little Charlie came forth in confession, then the other priests could not break their sacramental seal—tight-lipped."

"I think Detective Hickes would have known about the seal of secrecy, that it was going to make his case difficult to resolve."

Harry stood up from the table and picked up his report. "Let's go and eat. It's time for dinner."

"I'm not that hungry, Harry, but I will come to keep you company."

Harry smiled and said, "Sure, and let's bandage up your ankle to immobilize it ... just to be on the safe side."

While Harry went searching for the first-aid kit near the kitchen, Clarisse became tired of sitting and needed to stretch her leg. The resting position of her leg raised onto an adjacent chair was beginning to feel cramped. She raised herself by clamping onto the chair in front of her with both hands to offer support. Lifting herself with both arms, she turned her head slightly and captured an image in the corner of her eyes. It was Eleanor standing next to Little Charlie, holding his hand firmly like a proud auntie.

Clarisse jolted and lost her footing before she managed to soften her fall by sitting back in the chair with a bounce. She looked again, and they were two feet in front of her, having shifted from their original position instantly.

Clarisse shook her head, heart pounding. She flickered her eyes more than once to check. It wasn't her imagination.

They stood there, motionless, while Little Charlie grinned and Eleanor smirked.

Clarisse's blood pressure increased and made her feel like fainting.

Little Charlie shifted directly in front of her while Eleanor disappeared. He opened his mouth with wolf-like fangs and a red tongue grueling with green saliva as it wiggled out of his mouth. His eyes had become bloodshot red with a piercing look directed toward her.

Clarisse was phasing in and out as the image of Little Charlie became blurred and distorted.

Little Charlie had his hands around his neck marks while making a swirling motion, groaning and moaning like the howl of a dog.

Clarisse's mind finally gave way as it all became too much for her. She tilted her head forward and fainted onto the back of the chair. Her arm resting on the cushion of the chair next to her.

Harry managed to find the first-aid kit on the wall just outside the kitchen and came back to find Clarisse sprawled across two chairs. He dropped everything and dashed toward her immediately, concerned about her wellbeing.

"Clarisse? Clarisse, are you all right?" Harry was trying to stay calm, but his heart was racing. He tapped her on the face a few times gently to see if she would respond, and then he put his head on her chest to check that her heart was beating. He took her arm and checked for her pulse.

*Thank God she is breathing*, he thought.

He gently lifted Clarisse from the awkward position that she was resting in and removed her from the chair. He carried her to the sofa at the back of the dining room and placed her gently along the full length of the three-seater. She was breathing and did not appear to be in pain.

He tapped her again on the face with the tips of his fingers. "Clarisse, if you can hear me, everything is fine. Wake up, wake up."

There was no response, and she was motionless. Only a slight moan, and she moved her head from side to side.

"Clarisse, it's me—Harry. Wake up. Everything will be fine." Harry tapped her again on the face while he gently held her hand for reassurance.

Clarisse moaned again, but this time she partially opened her eyes. She looked groggy and out of it; however, she recognized Harry.

"Is that you, Harry?" she said faintly.

"Yes, it's me. You will be fine, Clarisse." Harry was doing his best to reassure her. "I'm not sure, but it looks like you fainted."

Clarisse blinked a few times and rubbed her forehead before shaking her head. "Where's Little Charlie? Has he gone?"

Harry was confused. Maybe the ordeal of searching for Little Charlie had affected her mind and she was hallucinating?

"There is no Little Charlie here," he said.

"Are you sure? I did see Little Charlie," Clarisse whispered convincingly.

"I promise he's not here." Harry caressed her hand while looking at her directly with concerned eyes.

"Little Charlie was different this time ... so different. He's not what you think he is."

Harry noticed a bump on her forehead from where she had hit it on the chair. "I better get you an icepack for your forehead."

Clarisse grabbed Harry by the arm before he took off and said, "Little Charlie is evil. Whatever happened to him when he was murdered changed him."

Harry looked directly at Clarisse and nodded. Now was not the time to express his opinion. He would leave that for another day.

# 8 THE HANDMAIDEN

Clarisse was thrust onto the basement floor on her side. The phantom hovered above the cobalt blue chest. She had taken it too far, and it had angered him. He did not like being challenged.

Little Charlie, with his wolf-like fangs and piercing red eyes held onto her ankle with his long fingernails clawed into her. It was painful as the nails penetrated deep into her skin.

"Let me go, you monster!" she yelled. She kicked profusely to release her legs from Little Charlie's grip, but he kept holding on, moaning like a dog in pain. She kicked him in the chest with her other leg, but it made no difference. He kept coming back more determined.

The phantom, angered by her resistance, started crushing the altar wine from the wine racks next to her, making them explode one by one. He was toying with her to test her stamina and faith.

Clarisse turned her head to avoid the broken shards of glass floating onto her face as they came piercing down on her. Her body was awash of red wine as it slid down her back like a stream.

"You're not the first or last person to challenge me!" the phantom said as he moved toward her. He had penetrating eyes and a pale white face with bulging veins along his cheeks.

Clarisse turned her head as he came toward her. It was a malevolent evil that had pervaded the basement, and Clarisse was no match. The evil force was too strong for her, and she could not repel it with her words or physical strength.

Little Charlie dug his claws into her ankles more deeply, and Clarisse screamed in pain. It was knifelike. Blood was starting to ooze out and absorbed into the dusty floor.

The horror was just beginning as she kept kicking him away, but each time Little Charlie became more aggressive. He thrived on the adventure and provocation.

In the chaos, Clarisse unscrewed the lid from a small glass bottle containing sacred holy water and splashed it all over Little Charlie. The boy screamed in pain and let go of her ankle as steam rose from his face. He retreated to the safety of the phantom and stood next to him as he looked on in surprise. Clarisse was prepared for the confrontation and had taken precautions.

The phantom, angered by her fight, lifted the wooden cross that was resting against the back wall. He catapulted it into midair and pointed it toward her. The tip formed into a sharp point, like a spear.

Clarisse panicked, putting her hand over her face as she waited for the phantom to propel it toward her. She shrieked a long, blaring cry.

"To hell with you, Grimaldi!" she yelled with intensity.

Determined that the phantom would not take her soul, Clarisse held onto her rosary beads and lifted both hands toward the piercing cross. It was her only defense, impromptu and probably pointless.

The cross hovered above her while the phantom raised his right hand in the air with arms extended. He was in control. All he had to do was give the word, and the cross would come down, stabbing through her heart.

Clarisse held the rosary beads above her head, praying to her God. If she were to die, it would be in God's hands.

The basement was the phantom's domain and so poisoned by evil that her prayers made no difference. He was unflinching and angered by her prayers.

He raised his other arm in the air, ready to give the command. It was the defining moment that would send the upside-down cross spiraling toward her heart. It sent a shrill through her body.

Clarisse woke from her bed, drowned in sweat and trembling. She had just had a bad dream, yet it had been so real that it took her a couple of minutes to get over it.

Harry had left early for the day to return to the worksite and continue working on his project, so she was alone.

Although her dream had startled her, she also believed there was meaning by recounting parts of it—symbols that could help her with clues to understanding the phantom's presence—no matter how painful it was.

She planned to continue the intuitive exploration of Paranormal Jack's archive boxes. A visit to the basement was on her list of things to do.

On her way to the basement, she tried to make sense of the symbols, such as the bursting of sacred wine bottles, blood, and an upside-down stabbing cross. She also recalled the holy water and how it had repelled Little Charlie. Was it something that could protect her in their presence?

Upon entering the basement room, the phantom wasted no time in engaging her in conversation.

"So, you have come back for more, my dear, when others would have run away," said the phantom. He was cross-legged with a pipe in hand, sitting on the cobalt blue chest.

Clarisse stood at the entrance of the room, undisturbed by his presence. "Curiosity brought me back, phantom … or should I say, Father Grimaldi?"

"Oh, Father Grimaldi does not live here anymore. He has long gone from this world."

"And you have decided to show yourself this time? Who are you then, phantom? Who do you represent?" Clarisse clasped her hands tightly to release the tension throughout her body. She was sweating uncontrollably.

"I am the devil, and I can take any form I wish. It helps me lure you away from your Creator and influence your psyche."

Clarisse waited as the phantom lit his pipe. "I want to know about Little Charlie. What happened to him?"

"But, my dear, haven't you been scrummaging through the files outside and not worked it out already? I did give a clue with the archive box number," the phantom said in a sarcastic tone.

"Oh yes, I know Detective Hickes' version, but I want to hear your explanation."

"You mean, what part I played in it?" The phantom laughed in a satirical way.

Clarisse was feeling anxious, wanting to push the phantom into explaining the truth about Little Charlie.

"You possessed the priest that ended Little Charlie's life, didn't you?" Clarisse took another step closer toward the phantom.

"The priest let down his guard and became careless. It made him vulnerable, so I saw the opportunity."

"The opportunity to do what, phantom?" Clarisse raised her voice.

"I don't possess souls, my dear. It is not necessary. All I need to do is poison you with the venom of hatred, despair, lust, and greed. Then the rest comes easily." The phantom stood up from the cobalt blue chest and pointed toward the rope hanging at the back of the wall.

"And what about that rope? I'm assuming you were looking for ways to lure the priest astray. That's your job, isn't it, phantom?" Clarisse said fervently.

"Ha-ha. You catch on nicely, my dear. But it was not hard with Father O'Leary. The man should never have become a priest, and he wore the robe for a different purpose. It was a vehicle to gain unlimited access to little boys, if you know what I mean."

Clarisse gulped at the thought that one of the priests in the presbytery had a history of child molestation.

"And rather than deal with it, your Church removed Father O'Leary from his post in Ireland and sent him to this outpost, where nobody would suspect a thing." The phantom smiled mordaciously. "That is your God ... and He did nothing about it."

There was dead silence in the room as Clarisse absorbed the wretched detail.

"So, you have lost your tongue, my dear? The truth hurts, doesn't it? Your God, the infallible one, could have saved Little Charlie and did nothing about it," said the phantom as he poked his tongue at her.

"But you pushed Father O'Leary into committing this crime."

"My dear, he did not need much convincing when I promised him all the fruits of the earth and everything he could ever imagine." His voice started to fade into the distance as the phantom slowly receded from view. "You may want to review box number six this time. Maybe you missed something?" The voice faded even further. "Number six."

The phantom vanished, and the vibrant light that radiated from the cobalt blue chest faded away, plunging the basement into darkness.

Clarisse could see rays of sunlight filtering from the stairs through a gap in the door and made her way toward it briskly, not wanting to show she was frightened or unnerved by the phantom. However, something was chewing at her feet, attempting to drag her back. She recognized the stench and the howling cries of a dying dog. It was Little Charlie taunting her again as she niggled at her shoes with his teeth.

"Oh, my dear, don't mind Little Charlie. Sometimes he behaves like a dog," said the phantom as his voice echoed across the room.

Clarisse kicked and struggled to release Little Charlie from her foot as she dragged him along the pavement. She was reaching for the safety of the door, her heart pounding throughout her body. Her adrenaline kicked into overdrive as she reached a state of heightened anxiety. She fought for her freedom as she clasped the door handle, holding it tightly with both hands as she kicked her leg frantically to release Little Charlie. But he would not let go and became fierce with every boot.

Clarisse opened the door and held onto the frame of the wall, propelling herself outside the room with one final, exalted push. Little Charlie let go and made his way back to the cobalt blue chest, to the safety of the phantom.

"Oh, my dear, that's what happens when you treat someone like an animal," said the phantom. His voice was everywhere, echoing throughout.

Clarisse looked back as she lay on the floor, gathering herself.

"And the next time you decide to visit, my dear, come

prepared ... Little Charlie and I will be waiting."

Clarisse was not worried about the threat from the phantom. She understood that was what phantoms did—made you worry and fearful. She had developed beyond that, and while most people would have panicked and run away, Clarisse was generally composed.

She stood up and dusted herself off while making her way to the basement staircase. She glanced over to Paranormal Jack's storage boxes and recalled the phantom referring to archive box number six. He had repeated it more than once, and she believed it meant something. It piqued her interest, so she decided to walk back down the staircase to look for it.

Clarisse did not waste any time shifting one box after another until she found archive box number six. It was not as well-assembled as the other boxes—a used cardboard package from a supermarket hastily put together with white tape. It had obviously been assembled in a hurry then left for storage.

She reached for her cutting knife then steadily opened it from one side, careful not to cut through the box too deeply. Once opened, she saw loose papers hurriedly put together with a paperclip. The documents were not filed sequentially. Clarisse needed more time to examine the contents, and the basement was not conducive to a thorough review.

She tried lifting the carton to test how heavy it was, finding it light enough to carry upstairs to the recreation room of the presbytery where she could scrummage through the documents.

An hour had passed as Clarisse meticulously examined every document. One thing was for sure—all the notes had belonged to Detective Hickes. How Paranormal Jack had managed to get ahold of his transcripts was unclear.

Caught between a pile of scrappy paper with handwritten notes, Clarisse found a document in perfect condition from the Archdiocese. It was a chronological record of service for Father O'Leary, containing his forced transfer to Australia.

Her eyes were glued to the transcript. She could not believe what she had exposed about the priest. It had been covered up by the church with allegations about the mishandling of children. Each time there had been an incident, Father O'Leary had been moved to another parish until it all got to be too much. The final entry, signed by the Archdiocese, had authorized a transfer to Australia. They wanted to be done with him and shift the issue elsewhere.

How much Father O'Hara had known about his prior

convictions was not clear.

Detective Hickes' investigation had extended beyond Hartley and the borders of Australia. He had been onto something significant and had gathered evidence that would have put Father O'Leary behind bars.

Clarisse turned the transcript over to find handwritten notes by Detective Hickes.

> *The bastards won't talk. They are closing ranks and defending O'Leary. Fucking sacred oath!*

As Clarisse continued sifting through another pile of creased paper, she stumbled upon an incredible find. It was a police report from the Dublin Constabulary, addressed to Detective Hickes. Contained in that report was damning evidence about the terrible crimes committed by Father O'Leary. The Dublin Constabulary had also suffered from the same problem as Detective Hickes—witnesses were not forthcoming. However, there was another revelation, a notation that Father Grimaldi was to lead an internal investigation, a secret mission. He would transfer to Hartley and conduct an undercover inquiry on the conduct of Father O'Leary and the rest of the clergy. His main objective was to obtain written confessions.

Hartley had become a bedrock of the Catholic Church's antipathy. Although they had been a clergy, they had lost their way.

Clarisse turned the page over to find another handwritten note from Detective Hickes.

*Unconfirmed paranormal phenomena and supernatural disturbances in the presbytery abound?*

Detective Hickes, although not the superstitious type, had acknowledged that there had been unexplained phenomena shrouding his investigation. An inexplicable evil had been driving the priest's behavior into committing diabolical acts. He could not get enough evidence to prosecute, but it was enough to cast doubt on several priests.

Eleanor silently paced into the recreation room, unbeknownst to Clarisse.

"Hello, my dear. Sifting through the boxes, I see." She had a gently, squeaky voice.

"Oh, hi, Eleanor. Didn't hear you come in."

"Oh yes, I get that a lot from people. Some call me Lightfoot Eleanor."

"I was just fixing this box together. I found it collapsed downstairs," said Clarisse, trying to deflect the conversation.

Eleanor walked up alongside her and picked up a document laying next to Clarisse. "Paranormal Jack built a big collection of history. He was probably our best historian."

"Yes, we enjoyed his tales about Hartley when we had the opportunity to meet with him. We were just getting to know him before he died."

"Have you found anything of interest in this pile of stuff?" Eleanor asked.

"Well, now that you mentioned it, I have found something about a certain priest—Father O'Leary. Do you know of him?" Clarisse sifted several papers laid out on the table. She was looking for the record of Father O'Leary from the Catholic Church. "Oh, finally, here it is," Clarisse said.

She turned around to show Eleanor, but the woman was gone. Clarisse was stunned by the speed she had left the room.

"Eleanor, are you there?" Clarisse called out more than once. However, she was nowhere to be found and gone with the stroke of a magician's wand, an incredible disappearing act.

Clarisse picked up the box and tucked aside two key documents concerning Father O'Leary, preferring to keep them as evidence. She had stumbled onto a new twist on the fate of Little Charlie. What crossed her mind, though, was that Paranormal Jack had known more than he had let on, keeping the interesting or more scrupulous stories of Hartley to himself.

She checked the time and realized Harry would be home in the next half hour. Clarisse put the archive box underneath the table, away from view, and then she made her way to the front porch. She sat on the chair, sitting adjacent to the English-style garden. The town was empty except for a couple of gardeners trimming the hedges and plants nearby.

Because of her fondness for flowers, mainly white jasmines, she opted for a quick stroll of the manicured flowerbeds on the side of the presbytery.

She strolled along the gravel pathway leading toward the flowerbeds directly facing the church. It was a well-maintained country garden with an established rose bed. The roses consisted of white, red, and yellow varieties, and the fragrance filled your nostrils. It was a pleasant, relaxing sensation to walk along the cultured plants.

A gardener was trimming the lavender shrub that had overgrown onto the pathways with his clippers. He preferred to do it the traditional way rather than use power tools.

"Good morning, miss. Nice day for a wander?" he said, clipping away at the dense shrub.

"It's a lovely garden," Clarisse responded. "I have been

here for over a month, and it's the first time I have appreciated it."

"We take wedding photos here occasionally. Got a wedding this weekend, and they have asked to take pics along this walkway facing the church." He looked toward Clarisse and said, "I would like to give you a rose clipping, but the wedding party might notice it missing."

"Oh, that's no bother." Clarisse put her nose gently above a red one. "It's a perfect fragrance."

"Yes, miss. It takes many years to get them into that shape."

"I wanted to ask you if you have seen Eleanor?"

The gardener looked perplexed. "Which Eleanor are you referring to, miss?"

"Eleanor, the caretaker of the presbytery," she said.

"Oh. I have been working here for years, and no Eleanor is looking after this place."

"Are you sure? Petite lady with short dark hair and a squeaky voice, in her seventies?"

"Positive. The only person who runs this place lives out of town." The gardener stood up and looked at Clarisse while holding his clippers with his large hands. "The owners only come out once a week to check on the staff and then leave. They don't stay long."

"Is there an Eleanor in town, perhaps? Someone new?"

"No one lives here. Anyone who works here is from out of town." The gardener went back to clipping the shrubs.

"Have a good day," said Clarisse.

"You, too, miss."

Clarisse turned back and started making her way to the porch, pondering the gardener's comments. Perhaps it was a case of mistaken identity, and he had gotten it all wrong? At the same time, he had appeared confident about who came in and out of Hartley, as he was a local who had been working in the town for some time.

She heard a ruffling of leaves behind her, like little footsteps running across the gravel. The sound was amplified.

She turned instinctively to see Eleanor holding the hand of Little Charlie. They smiled at her vibrantly, trying to draw her closer, waving her to come over. Her heart bolted, and she shook her head a couple of times. Her body shivered from the impromptu apparition.

*Can't be real*, she thought.

Rather than say anything and be lured into their evil conspiracy, she turned and kept walking. Clarisse did not want to engage with them, preferring the safety of the porch. She picked up the pace as her feet scraped along the uneven pathway. Step by step, kicking away tiny branches that lay in front of her. Her brisk walk turned into a light jog as she picked up the pace.

As she made her last turn around the rose bed, she saw the porch in front of her. Perspiring from the tension and adrenaline rush, she built the courage to look back once more. There was nothing there. Little Charlie and Eleanor were gone. Even the sound of the gardener's clipping had stopped. Only the wind blowing into the eucalyptus trees and shrubs could be heard whisking away in the background.

From the safety of the porch, Clarisse looked to the car park. There were no vehicles in sight. She glanced into the emptiness of the town. There was nothing around. Hartley was an abandoned ghost town. No sight of the gardener and his Ute or equipment near the presbytery, as you would expect from a maintenance person.

These encounters might have spooked several people into leaving town, but not Clarisse. It motivated her further to solve the puzzle of Hartley and the evil within.

At first, she had toyed with the prospect of unravelling its sinister history. Now, she had become absorbed by it. She had meddled so much into Hartley's unsolved past and uncovered a plethora of information that she could not let go. In a way, she was continuing what Detectives Hickes had left behind.

Clarisse had discovered what had defined Hartley in the

earlier years of settlement—an outpost Australian colonial town drowned in the sorrow of outcast priests with a sinister past. They had been prescribed with the care of orphaned young children in a derelict act of neglect so deprived that it handed the devil a way into compromising their faith. And what Detective Hickes had revealed was a mutiny of evil against the Church—Saint Bernard's Church had become a bastion of sin and embarrassment for the Holy See. So much so that they had to send one of their most trusted investigators to conduct an inquiry and report back his findings.

Against all the odds, Father Grimaldi had ground his way through the truth until he'd become a target of evil himself. The phantom had left him with no choice, but to trade his soul in a final testament of good versus evil.

## 9 THE OFFERING

Clarisse put down the archive box to inspect the noise in the room adjacent to her. The Victorian-style door handle leading to the phantom's room had clicked open as though someone was opening it from the inside. The worn door hinges made a screeching sound that almost perforated her eardrums.

She ground her teeth and closed her eyes momentarily to absorb the pitch. Clarisse knew what it meant—the phantom was inviting her inside for another conversation.

With one foot inside the room, she ducked her head between the gap in the door. The phantom was sitting on the cobalt blue chest, puffing on a pipe. He glanced toward her but did not say a word as he continued puffing. Sitting next to the phantom was Little Charlie, cross-legged and playing with a rope that had a hoop at the end. The circle was big enough to wrap around someone's head, and he continuously played out that motion, placing it around his neck, tugging on it, and then removing it. Little Charlie grinned toward Clarisse and waved at her.

"Is there something you want to ask me, my dear?" said the phantom.

Clarisse reflected on what to say. "I want to ask you about Eleanor, the caretaker."

"Oh, Eleanor, the handmaiden, you mean?"

"Is that what she is?"

The phantom baulked and laughed out loud with a sinister tone. "Well, yes, over eighty years ago, she was the handmaiden for the priest at the presbytery." He grinned as he displayed his wolf-like fangs. "But you should never put a beautiful young woman amongst young, deprived priests, my dear. She was much more attractive back then than the eighty-year-old woman of today."

"But she is not the caretaker of this lodge?" Clarisse asked, in a probing mood.

"Let me bring you into something that you have not considered," said the phantom with a bold grin.

Clarisse stood still and did not say a word, deciding to nod instead.

"I am Eleanor, just like I am the gardener. And this disguise of a detective with a pipe? I am that man, also."

"What do you mean?" Clarisse asked, thinking he was indulging in sarcasm again.

"I am whatever I want to be. I can take many forms." The phantom took a puff of his pipe and exhaled the smoke. "I am not bound by your earthly rules—one body, one soul."

"You are all these people?"

"Yes. When I want to be and depending on how much fun I want to have at the time." The phantom stood up and pointed to a set of garden clippers on the wall.

"You're pointing at garden clippers? Why?" Clarisse was confused.

"Yes, because if the moment arises and you go for a walk in the garden, I can be the gardener and speak to you."

"So, Eleanor doesn't exist?"

"Of course not ... Well, not in your world."

"But what about Little Charlie?"

Little Charlie raised his head with glowing red eyes and licked his lips with a long, luscious purple tongue.

"I had sympathy for the little boy. I did not occupy his soul, preferring to be his spiritual guide instead," said the phantom.

Clarisse was impressed by the phantom's level of explanation.

"So, what about that cobalt blue chest that you always sit on? You can't take the soul of a physical object?"

"Is that a question or statement, my dear?" The

phantom was annoyed. "This chest is the property of my master, and it's how he controls this game."

"It's a game? You have to amuse him?"

"How else does he get pleasure?" The phantom stood next to the chest and raised his right leg onto it.

"So, what's in the cobalt blue chest, phantom?" Clarisse was deliberately pushy.

"I thought you would come to that. And come to think about it, I don't know what took you so long. Ha-ha."

Clarisse was speechless and hesitant to respond.

"Do you want to know or not?" asked the phantom. He was poking at her with screwed-up lips.

"Yes, yes, of course."

"In this cobalt blue chest are the souls I have possessed over the last one hundred and fifty plus years. The list is long, and you would be surprised who I have managed to capture." He was buoyant and starting to show off.

"Can you be a more specific, phantom?" Clarisse asked.

"In this chest are the souls I occupy and can take form of whenever I want. If I get bored with one, I amuse myself and take another."

"Like Eleanor …"

"Yes, like Eleanor, although she is boring, and I usually prefer Father O'Hara. You can run amuck with those guys." The phantom grimaced.

Clarisse was shocked at the extent of his powers. It superseded anything she might have envisaged.

"What's the matter, my dear? Cat got your tongue?" The phantom was poking fun at her again.

"And the soul you occupy now? Who is he?" Clarisse inquired.

The phantom looked at her directly and took another puff off his pipe. "Oh, this is Detective Hickes. Like you, he could not resist the temptation for more information. He was the curious type. You remind me of him." The phantom stood up tall and put aside his pipe.

Clarisse swallowed in disbelief. "Detective Hickes?" she asked. She scorned at the thought that Detective Hickes had found his fate in the phantom's evil curse.

"Oh yes. And why not? He was a great choice."

Little Charlie stood up and dropped the rope on the floor. He clapped his hands in glee like a small child at a puppet show.

"What else is in the chest, phantom?" Clarisse crossed her arms and waited for a response.

"I like your intuition, my dear, but I think that is enough information for one day."

The phantom echoed into the distance then vanished from the room alongside Little Charlie. The glow of the cobalt blue chest faded until it became a rusty brown, derelict object.

"I hope all is well with your Harry..." said the phantom as a parting comment.

Clarisse understood the phantom never provided her all the information at once. Snippets at a time were his mantra to get her interested enough to return. He played on her curiosity and obsession into the paranormal to lure her back.

Clarisse rushed out of the room, almost losing her footing on the moisture that lined the floor's surface. She headed straight for her room to search the archive box containing Detective Hickes' investigation notes. She recalled a picture of him in front of Saint Bernard's Church.

She thrust the door open and scampered toward the archive box, almost falling over a pair of boots laying near the entrance. Harry was very untidy and hopeless in the morning with his routine, preferring to leave things for when he got back. It was a typical, I-will-do-it-later attitude.

Clarisse removed the lid from the archive box and turned it upside down, dropping all the papers onto the floor. She was impatient, wanting to sift through the documents quickly.

She shuffled through the pictures until she found it. Grabbing hold of the image with both hands, she saw it was a monochrome photo in excellent condition, typical of the times.

The picture was of Father Grimaldi standing next to Detective Hickes in front of Saint Bernard's Church. It was a significant find because, according to the transcripts from the investigation, Detective Hickes and Father Grimaldi had never met each other. The study had gone further than intended, and the Catholic Church had cooperated with the local police to investigate their parish priests in secrecy. It appeared they had shared information to help each other achieve their aim—to get to the bottom of the circumstances clouding the parish.

Clarisse kept looking for other documents that might have appeared perfectly normal that had not risen her awareness. She might have missed essential notes amongst the usual scribble.

She meticulously went through every document again, phrase by phrase, to find the critical links to the investigation. She searched for almost two hours before she found a creased page that appeared torn out of a notebook.

Clarisse read through the handwritten note by Detective Hickes. Her eyes cringed and heart palpitated with every sentence. She had found a significant connection.

> *Strange happenings found at the presbytery at night, and particularly in the basement. In the evening, bright lights flickering and noticeable from the steps of the church. On one occasion, in what appeared a priest gone mad, a so-called Father O'Leary wandering around the cemetery barefoot and in his undergarments. He mumbled aloud while holding his rosary as he fled to the safety of the church. The place seems bereft of an evil incarnation, an unexplainable source of madness within the ranks of the church.*
>
> *I will visit this basement tomorrow evening and conduct an inspection, but it must be when everyone is asleep. I don't want to announce my visit. The element of surprise is the most important.*
>
> *Senior Sergeant Hickes*

Harry was overdue from his day out in the field, so Clarisse waited patiently for his arrival for dinner in the empty restaurant. Once again, they would have the place to themselves.

Harry had informed her that they had one week to complete the project. Then they would be heading back to the hustle and bustle of Sydney and life of readjustment.

Clarisse decided that dinner would be a great time to tell Harry of her findings. She wanted to shed light on the story of Little Charlie, Father O'Leary, and the other discoveries that she had unearthed from Detective Hickes' investigation. She wanted to share her opinion about Paranormal Jack's car crash—that it was not an accident but an evil and sinister plot. However, she did not want to come clean on her interactions with the phantom, as Harry would consider it farfetched.

Being a skeptic, Harry would be prone to making his way into the basement to see for himself. Not because he was curious about the paranormal, but rather to prove her wrong—baseless with a wild imagination for the supernatural. Harry had accepted that Clarisse was wired this way because of her cultural upbringing. He made nothing of it and usually went along for the ride, often poking fun. As for Clarisse, she did not want to change him, either. In a way, they complemented each other with a balanced view.

Thirty minutes had passed, and no sign of Harry. He was never this late without calling Clarisse. She attempted to contact him several times on his mobile phone, but he was not answering.

She sat patiently on the porch, overlooking the main street to get a first glimpse of him driving into town. She was anxiously shaking her foot, which then progressed to her knees. It was a nervous reaction to release the tension as she began to worry.

In the distance, she noticed a white sedan driving into Hartley, but it was not Harry's car.

*Maybe his car broke down?* she thought.

The car pulled up at the car park in front of her. A man in his fifties wearing an embroidered shirt with the company logo jogged toward her. He looked worried and uneased, hopping over garden beds to reach her rather than take the pebble pathway to the front gate.

"Are you Clarisse?" he asked with a stoic face.

Clarisse did not like the look of his demeanor. Her stomach tightened, and she clasped her hands.

"Yes, I am Clarisse. Is everything all right?"

"Well ..." He was solemn and ready to deliver awful news about Harry.

"I'm the project manager at Harry's workplace. My name is Steve. Harry had an accident at work this afternoon. He collapsed, and we rushed him to the hospital in Lithgow."

Clarisse was frozen and shaking, fearing the worst.

"How is he now? Is he okay? Can I see him?"

"Harry is awake and under observation, but they won't release him until the tests are complete." He provided Clarisse with a card with the hospital details and the name of the doctor treating Harry. "You can call the hospital and find out when you can visit him and get an update on how he's progressing." He procrastinated then took out his business card. "This is my number. I can get a member of my team to take you to the hospital tomorrow if you like. It's no problem for us. All you need to do is contact me."

Clarisse was worried and insisted on seeing Harry immediately. However, the project manager suggested to leave it until the next morning.

"Does Harry know you're speaking to me?"

"Yes, he knows I'm here. He told me to tell you he's fine and not to worry."

"Oh. Are you sure I can't see him tonight?"

"Clarisse, best leave it alone for tonight and let's arrange it for tomorrow. He is well looked after by the hospital staff. I am on call anytime if you want to speak to me," he said reassuringly.

Clarisse sat back on the chair and watched as the white sedan left town. She was alone at the presbytery with nobody to talk to. She desperately wanted to speak to Harry, but at the same time, she tried to heed the advice of the project manager. It was getting dark, so it was not a good time to be driving around the countryside. And it was a forty-five-minute drive to Lithgow through winding roads that were not well maintained. The trip to Lithgow at night was best left to the expertise of the locals who understood the dangers on the road.

Clarisse cancelled her dinner at the restaurant, preferring to eat alone in her room.

She was not done with the phantom, and she recalled the apparition making a side comment about Harry. It had meant nothing to her at the time, and it had not registered anything significant. She planned to head back to the basement and find out more. There was something the phantom was not informing her about, and she wanted him to come clean.

Clarisse bolted to the basement with an intense determination and disregard for the phantom. She was not afraid of his antics, mind games, or cynicism.

"And what brings you back, my dear? I sense a problem," said the phantom. He was sitting in his usual pose, wearing the detective's long jacket and hat.

Clarisse was defiant and not in a mood for a chat. "You know about Harry, don't you?"

"Oh yes, I know everything, whether it's now or in the

future."

Next to the phantom stood Little Charlie, playing with picture cards, and Eleanor, wearing a handmaiden's uniform. Eleanor's complexion was fifty years younger. She was a beautiful woman with luscious dark hair tied in a bun and wore rosy red lipstick to complement her audacious smile.

"So, it looks like you have brought everyone with you this time. Your entourage?" Clarisse said sarcastically.

"Ha-ha. I believe you call it a team these days. We work together."

Clarisse stepped forward with intent. She wanted to show no fear. "You already knew Harry would end up in the hospital last time we spoke?"

"Well, that should not come as a surprise to you, should it?" The phantom puffed on his pipe then exhaled, sending a plume of smoke straight toward her face. "I know everything about everything," he proclaimed.

Clarisse waved her hand in front of her to disperse the smoke away and coughed.

"I suppose it's one of your games again?"

"Well, you could see it that way. I do try to make them interesting each time, add a different twist. Otherwise, it would get boring, my dear." The phantom stood up with red eyes focused on her. "I can make you a deal, if you like?"

Clarisse crossed her arms and stood firm, unperturbed by his devilish look. "What deal?"

"Let me put it this way. Doctors don't know where to look, and they will misdiagnose Harry."

"And you know the diagnosis?"

"Oh yes, and I know how to save him." The phantom reached for the cobalt blue chest and unlocked the bolt. "It's all in here, my dear—the prognosis on his health and the remedy. It's all in the chest."

"How can I believe you, phantom? Remember, it's a game for you? How do I know you won't change the rules?" Clarisse asked.

"Oh yes, well, if you thought I was going to help your Harry for nothing in return, then you're misguided."

Little Charlie giggled, and Eleanor sighed.

"It's always a tradeoff for you, phantom. You play with our lives for your enjoyment and nothing else."

"Is there something wrong with that? It's what I do." The phantom's voice echoed across the room in a display of enthusiasm.

"So, what is the deal, phantom?"

"Aha, I knew you would come to your senses." The phantom looked toward Eleanor and Little Charlie and sent them away. "It's just you and me now. So, here is my proposal."

There was an uneasy silence. The phantom disappeared then reappeared again, tapping Clarisse on her shoulder with a slender, elongated arm. The long fingers and pointed fingernails pinched her skin with the force of a needle prick.

"Ouch!" Clarisse cried as she turned toward the entrance of the room. It was a middle-aged man with a long beard and captain's cap, reminiscent of eighteenth-century sailing ships. An overcoat and shiny black boots completed the apparition.

"And who are you now, phantom?" she asked. "Is this a new character in your game?"

"I was getting bored with Detective Hickes … Time for a change. This is Captain Tobias Aldershot of the convict ship, *The Eudora*. I thought you would like the embodiment of the man who discovered Hartley. He is the owner of the cobalt blue chest."

"You managed to get his soul like the others, I assume?" Clarisse was playing along with his diversion.

"I'm not here to give you a history lesson, my dear." The phantom placed his index finger on his forehead and thought about his next response.

"Was Captain Aldershot the ship's master?"

"Oh yes, but you can call me Captain if you like." The

phantom adjusted his white cap featuring a black brim with gold cord trim.

"Are you going to tell me how you possessed his soul?" Clarisse insisted.

"If you want to know ... Upon the completion of his contract with the New South Wales Governor, he was granted an allotment of land and named it Hartley. He brought his cobalt blue chest with all his prized possessions and established himself as a successful grazer in the area." The phantom walked a couple of steps and crossed his arms. "So, how is that for a history lesson?"

Clarisse had a quaint look on her face as she waited for the phantom to elaborate.

"They forgot to tell him the land was an aboriginal sacred site, and that's when all the problems began." The phantom laughed. "I suppose nothing is for free, and it was land no one wanted."

Clarisse placed her arms on her hips. She wanted to explore further. "Are you suggesting this hill where the presbytery was built is sacred indigenous land?"

"Yes, my dear, and the spirits were not happy." The phantom floated across the room to his usual spot on the cobalt chest. "It's not good to upset the spirits of the land. It can land you in trouble, especially these types. They are not that nice."

The phantom appeared to be reveling in his new embodiment. He caressed his beard several times by stroking it in a downward motion with his fingers. He adjusted his captain's hat firmly on his head in the image of the master of a ship.

Clarisse was starting to tire of his history lesson and dialogue. She wanted to know how to help Harry, whose condition would begin to worsen.

"Can we go back to Harry and talk about the deal you want to make?"

Her comment angered the phantom. He moved toward the ceiling with his feet inverted like a centipede against the wall. He stood there, looking at her like a mountain lion ready to pounce, an evil stare that penetrated your skin and touched your heart with fear.

"So, you want to save your darling Harry and make a deal with me?" The phantoms voice bounced off the solid walls and reverberated repeatedly.

Clarisse put both hands over her ears to soften the impulsive sound. "Yes," she replied. "Yes!"

The phantom walked down the side of the wall with his body arched and head poking out. It was not in proportion.

Clarisse jolted, her heart pounding as an intense shiver took over her body. She closed her eyes and shrieked.

"I have a deal for you," said the phantom, and he

stopped in his tracks just above the cobalt blue chest. "My master wants me to do something different this time—entertain him with a twist. He is starting to get bored with me taking over souls randomly."

"What is your proposal?" Clarisse asked.

A single lamp hanging from the ceiling flickered on and off, making her lose sight of the phantom.

"You inherit my power for five days and use it any way you want."

"You are testing my loyalty versus greed and power?"

The phantom was silent as he resumed his usual position on the cobalt blue chest, legs crossed and with a captain's pipe again.

"Are you going to answer me?" she asked.

"Oh yes, my dear, it's the greatest test of all. Your love for Harry versus all the greed for the material world and the power to control your destiny. You will have all the wealth and riches that you desire, limitless and beyond your dreams."

Clarisse was played-off. It was the devil's game to test her unrepenting love for Harry.

"And what happens after the five days? Another one of your tricks come into play, phantom?" Clarisse crinkled her forehead and stared purposely.

"Oh no, my dear. Even devils have contracts." He

pulled out a document from his chest. "This contract would ensure that, after five days, you can walk away from your obligations. Call it a disclaimer, if you like."

"What about Harry?"

"Harry will remain healthy and not get sick again." The phantom held out his arm with the document. "It's all in the disclosure at the bottom of the page."

Clarisse hesitated, not knowing if the phantom was playing an elaborate game. "I need to think about it."

"Why is that, my dear?"

"You don't exactly have a reputation for being true to your word—trickery is your game," said Clarisse.

The phantom chuckled and smiled back. "Now, now … No need to be like that. I will leave the contract on the cobalt chest. Take it, read it, and make your own decision." The phantom took another puff off his pipe. "However, don't take too long, because Harry is only going to get worse by the day. Time is of the essence, my dear."

The phantom slowly faded away, and so did the cobalt blue chest as it reverted to a rusty brown, worn-out trunk. The stench that generally occupied the basement was gone with the evil presence that accompanied the phantom. It was a standard basement room again.

## 10 THE COBALT CHEST

Clarisse had reached an agreement with the phantom and the devil, as his subsidiary. The phantom agreeing to five days for Clarisse to make up her mind was a stroke of genius. The phantom had to appease the devil, and what better way than to turn it into a game? It was a game of hedging based on an assumption. The power in the cobalt blue chest would be so paramount that no mortal could walk away. That meant Clarisse would be locked in forever as the new devil's plaything if she accepted after five days.

Harry was in the hospital recovering; the mystery illness diagnosed to be a rare infection. The doctors had found the cause and treated him with a spectrum of antibiotics.

Her deal with the devil had been underwritten. If, after five days, Clarisse decided not to become the bearer of his eternal powers, Harry would not get sick again, and his health would be assured.

But what was in the cobalt blue chest that held the

phantom captive? What remarkable power did it possess?

Her agreement with the phantom required she visit the cobalt blue chest in the basement at least three times to explore its contents. She thought it best to get this arrangement underway as soon as possible. Clarisse had no intention of inheriting the powers of the phantom. It was a deal solely for the purposed to get Harry back to health.

Clarisse waited for the last couple to leave the wedding entourage on Monday morning from the presbytery. She didn't want prying eyes around when she made her way to the basement for her first exploration of the cobalt chest. The weekend had been busy with more weddings than usual at Saint Bernard's Church.

Clarisse was in the basement, hesitating at first to enter the room. She was showing remorse, knowing she had made a pact with the phantom and the devil, possibly trading her soul forever. This was despite her beliefs—that all her life, her family had practiced superstition to ward off demons and evil spirits from their lives. It went against her grain. However, she'd had no other options. The pact with the phantom was to ensure Harry's recovery; that was the deal.

The room had a different feel to it. None of the anger that the phantom had displayed in the past. The putrid smell of arsenic and rotting flesh was gone. The rope hanging on the wall and the garden clippers that Little Charlie had played with was missing. Even the sun's rays managed to filter from the rooftop basement window where many light shows could be seen from the outside at night. The flickering lights from the solitary hanging lightbulb had ceased. It was a typical basement room, and if you were unaware of the evil that resided within it, it would come across as an ideal cellar.

In the corner of the room was the cobalt blue chest made of iron with large rivets to hold it together. It was in pristine condition, as though never handled, straight out of the craftsman's workshop. No signs of marks, scratches, or indentations that you would expect from a chest transported on an eighteenth-century sailing ship for thousands of miles. It was what made this chest so mysterious. It had a large mortice lock around the handle that kept it secured. The mortice lock was more of a prop than anything else, a disguise to give it a natural look, as no one could get into the chest without the permission of the phantom. A crowbar or jackhammer could not dislodge the mortice lock. It would bounce off with each impact without leaving an indentation.

Clarisse steadily walked toward the chest, calm at first, but growing with tension at every step. She had been conditioned to expect a paranormal sideshow from the phantom, but there was nothing, and it bothered her. It was not like the phantom to be this quiet.

The mortice lock dislodged in front of her—*click, click*—and fell to the floor. The sound of the impact bounced off the walls and filled the room with an echo.

She looked around, expecting the phantom to appear and partake in his usual taunts. Not this time. There was nothing but dead silence.

She placed her hand on the chest handle, hesitated, and looked around the room. The sound of heart thumping and constriction overtook her body as she procrastinated. Then, as Clarisse tugged open the chest, it became stuck. *Tug, tug, tug.* She pulled once more with on almighty attempt until finally releasing it.

Peering over the chest and into its contents, she was amazed by its pristine condition—a polished cobalt metal that appeared as though human hands had never touched it.

Inside the chest were a couple of items of curiosity. Clarisse picked up the rope that Little Charlie played with and fiddled with it with both hands. It was two inches thick with a noose at the top and dried bloodstains that had tainted it red. Clarisse didn't feel at ease holding the rope that supposedly was used to end Little Charlie's life. She tried to put it back in the chest but couldn't as it clung to her.

Clarisse shook her hands rigorously in a panic to oust the rope. Bloodstains started to penetrate her sleeves. The bloodstains were not fake, and they felt fresh, cold, and slithery, as it encroached onto her skin and up her arms. Again, she tried to dislodge the rope, but it clung on like plastic wrap. She felt dizzy and swayed side to side, almost losing consciousness.

Clarisse was taken back to the moment when Little Charlie had met his fate at the hands of Father O'Leary. She could not move, frozen as the chimera played out in front of her.

It was a devasting imagery of horror and pain as Father O'Leary held Little Charlie firmly across his chest with his forceful arms as the boy screamed and kicked in fear of his life. It was at the back of the presbytery, next to the pond and big eucalyptus tree. It looked different than the present—perfectly manicured English gardens with lavender shrubs in full-bloom lining the side of the banks of the pond.

Father O'Leary continued his struggle with the boy as the fear in Little Charlie's eyes and cries for help went unanswered. Clarisse could feel the torment of the six-year-old boy and desperately wanted to save him. Tears rolled down her cheeks as she reached out with her arms.

"Hold onto my arms, Charlie!" she yelled.

Little Charlie turned toward Clarisse and put out his tiny arms, crying and screaming, "Help me! Help me!"

Father O'Leary appeared dismissive of her presence, as though Clarisse was not there. He tied the noose around Little Charlie's neck and tightened it quickly. Father O'Leary was in a fit of rage as he screamed to his God, begging forgiveness repeatedly.

"Mea culpa, mea culpa," he said, bloodguilt.

He tightened the rope around Little Charlie's neck then threw the other end over a stable branch above. He tugged and tugged on the rope, lifting Little Charlie from the ground slowly until his tippy toes could no longer feel the ground.

Clarisse screamed, "No! You bastard of a priest, let the boy go!" She tried desperately to reach for him again, but it made no difference.

With each pull of the cord, Little Charlie coughed, spurted, and cried tears of pain as his face turned bright red from the lack of oxygen. Father O'Leary lifted him farther off the ground, in an uncontrollable rage

"No, no!" Little Charlie cried one last time. "I want my mummy!" he said as he choked. They were his last words before giving way to death as he exhaled his last tiny breath.

His legs stopped kicking, the air from his tiny lungs emptied, and his head tilted to one side as he lost consciousness.

And although he was an orphan, calling for mummy was his only sense of comfort—the final thoughts of an orphan boy who understood he once had a mother.

Little Charlie was dead. He had been the victim of an insane priest not fit to be a man, let alone a servant of God.

Clarisse was back next to the cobalt blue chest and in tears. She let go of the rope and put her hands over her face, head down. She was sensitive to young children and their welfare. It was an immense pain to feel the last moments of an innocent little boy, defenseless and on his own. His only crime was to be an orphan and placed in the care of a mentally ill priest, in an institution that had failed to protect him.

"Is that it, phantom? Is that the best you can do?" Clarisse yelled into the empty room. "Your chest of goodies is nothing but a living hell of bad recollections!"

But the phantom was not there and disinterested in her hurtful respite. It was what she had signed up for, and there would be more to come. It was a game, and her pain was his gain—to watch her suffer as she confronted all the evil of Hartley, one by one. Those were his intentions.

Clarisse took a few minutes to gather herself after the

traumatic experience of witnessing Little Charlie's death, coming to terms with what she had signed up for and understanding the significance of her agreement with the devil.

Peering over the chest once more, she lifted a black handmaiden's dress with a white collar made of a beautiful embroidery. It was in perfect condition and expertly folded. It was made of the finest cotton as her hands glided across the expertly woven material.

Fearing another vision, she placed the dress back into the chest, but it was too late. The dress clung to her, and she could not let it go. She tried shaking it off her hands, but it would not dislodge from her grip. Her eyes became drowsy, and she could not control her movements, succumbing to the evil spirit's vision once again.

This time it was not Father O'Leary but a different priest—Father O'Hara. In a dark room, lit by a solitary oil lamp, the handmaiden struggled as she repeatedly attempted to push him away from his advances. Each time she defended herself with force, Father O'Hara became more aggressive, coming back at her harder and harder. His slippery tongue, drunk from intoxication, slithered and drooled over her. He minced his words like a drunken sailor as he attempted to rip off her dress.

Clarisse recognized the woman's face. It was Eleanor,

the caretaker. She was beautiful, with a slender body and felicitous face that made men fight and gall over her. A rare and prized beauty in a town devoid of any ladies of significant appeal. She was the Aphrodite of Hartley. She had thought she was safe working in the orphanage but had underestimated the filth and sexual desires of Father O'Hara.

Eleanor kicked and screamed out for help as she fought back from the priest's advances. One kick, then another, as they landed on the Father O'Hara's hips. He was hurt from the impact of her boot but continued, unperturbed. She was desperate to maintain her dignity.

His rage increased with every attempt until he managed to grip the handmaiden's dress and rip it from the waist down.

His tongue slithered, and his eyes drooled over her. "Come on, my dear … just a little fun for a solitary man of the cloth. I promise God will reward your services," said Father O'Hara.

Eleanor kept fighting back until she kicked the oil lamp from Father O'Hara's hand, sending the flame directly onto his clothing. He was on fire and in a fit of rage, helplessly waving his arms while trying to pat out the fire on his trousers. Tiny embers of smoke billowed into the air as he managed to prevent himself from catching fire by patting it out frantically.

Filled with immense anger, he then lunged toward Eleanor with both hands around her neck, choking her in a frantic fit of rage. She fell to the ground, and he lost his grip. He was much bigger than Eleanor and more robust as he tried to overpower her again by applying more pressure around her neck. She kicked and punched him in a frantic attempt to defend herself. But she had no strength left as the ordeal wore her down, bit by bit.

An iron candleholder lay next to her, and she picked it up, lunging it across his back. Father O'Hara gasped in pain from the impact.

"Nuh-uh," he scolded.

He rolled over then got himself up again while slipping on a patch of oil from the lamp that had dripped onto the floor. Father O'Hara was in immense pain as he limped toward Eleanor, who was hyperventilating and gulping for air from the trauma. Red in the face and begging for her life, her final attempts to push him away waivered.

Father O'Hara lunged for her neck again and commenced choking her while he positioned his body between her legs to hold her down.

Clarisse was in intense pain to save Eleanor and reached out for her. "Take my hand, Eleanor!" she yelled. "Take my hand!"

But, although Clarisse could see everything that was going on, they had no sense of her presence. Unlike Little Charlie who had been able to connect with her during his ordeal, the devil made sure that was not an option this time. Watch and suffer was his mantra. That was part of the devil's game.

Eleanor the Handmaiden was dead at the hands of a drunken priest, cursed by his uncontrollable sexual urges.

Clarisse had had enough of the cobalt chest and let go of the handmaiden's dress while attempting to slam the chest shut. It was stuck, and each time she applied more force, there was resistance. She tried with both hands to solicit more strength, but it made no difference. Someone was holding it back, a signal that her job was not done.

In the corner of the chest was a deerstalker cap worn by detectives in the eighteenth century that would have belonged to Detective Hickes. It was made of cotton with six triangular panels and lined in satin. Clarisse picked up the cap and patted the fabric to get a feel for the woven construction.

Within an instant, she was in the vestry of Saint Bernard's Church where the priests would change into the ceremonial gowns. Two priests stood at the door, one with a rifle and the other with a pitchfork. Detective Hickes stood at the opposite corner of the room, with his revolver locked on the priests. It was a standoff.

The priests were in a rage of fury as they cursed profanities at Detective Hickes while waving their weapons with threatening gestures.

"Lay down your weapons, or I will shoot!" said Detective Hickes, knowing his life was in danger.

"How dare you accuse us of the death of Little Charlie in our sacred place of worship. You have no respect for our Lord!" Father O'Leary was furious.

"You are charged for the murder of Little Charlie, and you will be taken into custody!" Detective Hickes proclaimed as he pointed to both priests.

Father O'Leary pointed the rifle directly at Detective Hickes, poking it forward. "You want to arrest us? And what proof do you have, other than what you heard?"

"It was you, Father O'Leary, who confessed the murder during your penance. Why don't you hand yourself in and be done with it?"

"I am not confessing to anything, especially not to you … You're not my God."

"And do you think your God would approve of what you have done?" said Detective Hickes, standing firm with his revolver directed at Father O'Leary. "Now, I'm asking you one last time to drop your weapons!"

It was a game of cat and mouse, a fresh-eyed encounter

between the priests and Detective Hickes.

Father O'Leary took two steps forward, pointing his rifle directly at the detective. "Forgive me, Lord—"

"Stop there right now and don't take a step closer or I will shoot." Detective Hickes was on the brink. He needed to act quickly in defense of his life.

Father O'Leary took another two steps forward and fired the rifle at Detective Hickes from close range.

As the detective fell backward to the ground, he instinctively fired his handgun, driving a bullet directly into Father O'Leary's chest. Now they had both taken devasting shots to the chest.

They rolled on the ground, gasping for air with life-threatening injuries. The blood leaked onto the floor in pools of red as it made its way toward the other priest, who dropped his pitchfork and ran out of the vestry, crying for help, panic-stricken from the diabolical incident.

Clarisse wanted to attend to Detective Hickes but could not. She was only there to witness the wrath of evil that existed within the church. That was the phantom's ploy—to make a point that her God had abandoned them.

Clarisse was back at the cobalt blue chest as she pondered the incident. It had been so real, as though in the room together with the protagonist. For now, the recollections of the past events had ceased.

On top of the chest was a note in a white envelope with a custom, single-waxed seal from Captain Aldershot. It looked formal and typical of the way people corresponded in the eighteen hundreds.

She took the envelope like a bat out of hell and steadily made her way out of the basement. She had had enough for one day and wanted out.

This time, she was not thrust into another scene as a witness. She had completed her quota for the day.

Sitting on the front porch with her legs extended onto another chair, she enjoyed the mild evening sun that filtered over the furniture. She lay back with the letter from Captain Aldershot and slowly peeled away the wax stamp with a knife. The time for hesitation was over. It was the right moment to read the contents. Whether good or bad, she wanted to know.

She thought about Harry recovering in the hospital. She missed him very much. If all went well with his improvements, he could be home in a couple of days. In the meantime, she was living a solace life in a ghost town with very little to do. Boredom was only a stone's throw away.

While carefully opening the old English-style envelope and crafted paper, she questioned the root of the nefarious possession attributed to Captain Aldershot. Had he transcended into a battle with the evil spirits of the land? Had the chest always been this way, or had it transformed into a sinister depository of evil when he had moved to Hartley? Clarisse hoped the letter would provide some answers.

Handwritten in old English style with the ink of a free-flowing fountain pen, it leaked of ink blots on the note.

> *To whom this letter will behold,*
>
> *I am Captain Tobias Aldershot of the convict ship, The Eudora. You have access to my cobalt blue chest from the evil phantom. It contains contents with immense power well after I have departed from this earth.*
>
> *I have been fighting a curse on sacred indigenous land that has been here for thousands of years. I have upset the spirits, but I do not give up my Christian battle to purge the malevolent force from this place and restore the land to our Holy Father.*
>
> *The evil spirit that possesses this land will engage you in trickery and mastery at every step. It will captivate you in games and believing it can offer you everything that our*

*Lord, Jesus Christ, cannot. But before you witness prosperity and future wealth, you will go through a journey of debauchery and malignant exposed by the abomination.*

*You are probably wondering why the demon did not remove this letter? This letter is coveted in sacred ink and wax that no man can asunder. Only the hand of God has the power to remove it. This letter serves you as a warning, but it will be your inner strength and faith in God that will decide your faith.*

*God bless you,*
*Captain Tobias Aldershot*

Clarisse put the letter down and pondered the message. Hartley had been a cesspool of evil right from the first day of settlement. A scared site on indigenous land for more than a thousand years, the community had never stood a chance. And while the Catholic Church and its missionaries had attempted to reclaim the area in the name of God, the evil that resided within had pecked them off one by one. It was a case of priests going mad and exporting their inner desires in an uncontrollable environment amongst hapless people.

Hartley, in its heyday, had been primed with virulent

sin amongst its population. It would have been full of temptation, even for an outpost of the Catholic Church and its priests. The evil that resided on the sacred land they called Hartley had made sure of it.

Clarisse had made a pact with the devil for five days with a get-out-alive clause. However, she had to endure the daily visions of the cobalt chests on three occasions. That was the devil's game—to see the manifestations for her reactions. It was like a sport, a form of entertainment.

Clarisse jolted from the chair, making it tumble over and onto floor. She realized that, in the basement, was an archive box containing material on Captain Tobias Aldershot. Paranormal Jack had traced the history of Hartley back to an early settler. It was worth going through the contents to learn more about this man and his fate.

She folded the letter and put it in her side pocket as she made her way back to the basement at a brisk pace. She was determined to find more clues to unravel the history of Hartley's evil possession.

While inside the basement, she removed the upper layer of archive boxes as they were stacked four rows high. The boxes with the numbers one through five were at the bottom of the stack. She needed to get to them first.

Clarisse was frantic and, on a mission, persistent and

purposeful. Finally, she found archive box number one, where it had all started. She cut the tape off the box with the Stanley knife then lifted the dusty cover.

Archive box number one was uncharacteristically different from all the other boxes—smaller and made of old eighteenth-century corrugated cardboard and pleated paper. It felt more robust and compact than the other archive boxes.

Clarisse took a grip of the box from both sides and unwaveringly made her way up the creaky basement stairs to her room. She did not want to inspect the contents in the basement because the light was insufficient.

She was puffing from the exertion, and her arms started to feel sore from the strain. Clarisse took a deep breath and shook her hands to release the muscle tension. Then she tipped the box upside down and dislodging the contents onto her small desk with haste.

There was a captain's hat, a pipe, and a badge from the Eudora. Captain Aldershot had started his career in private shipping lines before transferring to convict transport with the lure of greater rewards. There were documents of the land title from the New South Wales Governor and monochrome photos. The photos took her interest immediately as she lay them out in front of her in a row. Five photos altogether of Captain Tobias Aldershot.

There was one photo in particular that called for her attention—a pose of Captain Tobias Aldershot standing next to someone familiar.

Clarisse shook her head, blinked a few times, and then looked again, and again.

*It can't be?* she thought.

She picked up the photo and held it up to the light to get a better resolution. Her hand was shaking uncontrollable at the thought of what she was seeing. It was Paranormal Jack dressed in a black robe, standing on the hill that would one day become Saint Bernard's Church. On the back of the photo, it had an inscription: *1836 with my dear friend Jack.* The monochrome photo had been taken over one hundred and fifty years before Paranormal Jack's recent death?

Clarisse took a deep breath and held her hands together near her lips. She looked straight ahead with a blank expression as she pondered if that was the same Paranormal Jack or a pure coincidence. Her mind switched into the forensic mode as she gathered all the most recent photos of Paranormal Jack to check on the similarity. To her dismay, every picture of Paranormal Jack had his face blotched out.

So, who was Paranormal Jack? Was it another of the phantom's rapporteur of characters to play with minds, a trickery, a misleading to create confusion? She didn't know who to trust and believe anymore. As the phantom would put it: the people she had encountered during her stay at Hartley were either here, there, or everywhere.

Clarisse sifted through the contents of the box again, frantically looking for a clue. The belief drove her. There must have been something that explained Paranormal Jack's presence in the photo.

*I need to slow down, or I am not going to find what I need,* she thought.

Finally, she came across a crumbled piece of paper, handwritten by the Archdiocese of Dublin. It was no wonder she had missed it prior, as it was caught between other documents. The letter was clear as to who the person was—Father Jack McAuliffe. It was a transfer to Hartley town, and unlike the other priests stationed at the presbytery, Father Jack had been educated and from a wealthy background.

Was Paranormal Jack the embodiment of Father Jack McAuliffe or a descendent? Was the road death of Paranormal Jack somehow related or a pure coincidence?

# 11 THE VISION

Harry was in his hospital bed all on his own. He was not allowed visitors since doctors were concerned that the diagnosed infectious disease could affect others. It was a repentant infection that his body had succumbed to—persistent, stubborn, and with the risk of coming back. The doctors had misdiagnosed him in the beginning until they had found the culprit—a rare pathogen that required a substantial range of antibiotics. He was still on a drip, though besides feeling lethargic, he was getting better every day. The worse was over, and he looked forward to his homecoming with Clarisse.

As the evening descended into night, he could sense the sun setting outside. His window faced the side of the hospital where it captured the intense rays of the sunset, turning his room into a soft yellow ambience. It made him feel good to experience nature's beauty every evening, and he appreciated it even more since his hospital confinement.

He could only read a couple of pages of his book before it started to hurt his eyes, so he laid down his novel on the side table.

As he adjusted his pillow and accustomed his posture, he was drawn to an apparition in the corner of his room, sitting on the solitary visitor's chair. Next to the phantom was Little Charlie, playing with his rope as he smiled and mimed children nursery rhymes to pass the time.

Harry blinked, thinking the antibiotics were making him hallucinate, but the apparition did not go away. Although he was initially startled, he was not scared. It was not the first time he had encountered a ghost, and being a skeptic, he found them to be a challenge.

"Good evening, my dear sir," said the phantom. He was puffing on a cigarette and wearing his captain's hat.

"Who are you?" Harry asked.

"Oh, I can be anyone you want me to be. Let us see … perhaps I can be a detective or a handmaiden? I can be a priest, if you like!" The phantom turned on his side and crossed his leg. "But I must admit, Captain Aldershot is my favorite."

"What about the boy next to you? Why is he playing with a bloodstained rope?"

"Oh, you mean Little Charlie? His story is a long one. I will explain it to you one day." The phantom hugged Little

Charlie and smiled. "He is entrusted in my care because your God did a terrible job of looking after him!"

Harry was having trouble following the phantom's remarks but decided to go with the flow. He did not have the benefit of the research that Clarisse had uncovered at the presbytery.

"So, Clarisse has not mentioned anything about me?" said the phantom.

"Was she supposed to?" Harry was defiant.

"No, not really. But the reason you are alive, dear sir, is because of her. She saved your life."

"How?"

"By making a deal with me, of course. A contract for five days, if you like."

"A contract with you?" Harry was confused.

"Oh, and don't worry; your health is secured, I promise you."

"What do you mean?"

"She may find her newly acquired powers difficult to let go, once you start to see all the benefits, that is."

"She wouldn't make a contract with the devil—I know her too well," said Harry defiantly.

"No one else has the power to save you, and do you think your God was going to come to your rescue?" The phantom inhaled on his cigarette then sent a plume of circular smoke toward Harry.

Harry waved his hands to disperse the smoke, although the apple fragrance that made up the tobacco blend smelled good. It was bearable as it filled his room with the scent.

"Can you tell me why she would make a deal with you?" Harry was deliberately testing the phantom.

"Because she had no choice and realized it was the only way to save you. But in return, I gave her five days to try my powers that reside within the cobalt chest, to show her the good and the bad of what I can offer." The phantom took another puff off his cigarette while Little Charlie giggled in the background. "Of course, we start with the visions of horror before moving onto the visions of luxury, wealth, and grandeur. People always remember the latter, don't they?" said the phantom.

"You're going to pass on your curse without her knowing what she is getting herself into?" Harry asked in a wayward manner.

There was dead silence in the room before the phantom stood up and pointed toward Harry. "You catch on quickly, my friend. You see, it's time for me to pass the baton onto someone else. I have been doing this for hundreds of years, and there are other things I would like to do with myself."

"You are setting her up, aren't you?" Harry raised his

voice then coughed as the tension became too much for him.

"I'm fair this time. I'm giving Clarisse a choice after five days. An option I did not have when I accepted this wretched job from my predecessor," said the phantom.

"You're selling her a life of grandeur tied up in a web of evil." Harry sat upright in his bed and raised his hand to make a point. "She is too smart for that and will realize your trickery!"

"No need to get upset, Harry. It's not good for your recovery. Either way, whatever decision she makes, your recovery is assured ... no matter what." The phantom took one final puff off his cigarette and smiled.

Harry, starting to feel the pain through his body, laid back on the pillow as his encounter with the phantom had drained him.

"What sort of life will she have with you, Harry? Let's get straight to the point. You will have a mortgage, children, and will always be counting your money to get ahead of everyone else. That is capitalism. You will struggle all through your life until you retire. And finally, when you do have some money, you are too old to enjoy it. Illness, pains, and intolerance—you don't have the same enthusiasm for things anymore. Everything is so hard, and then you die in an aged care facility ... all on your own."

The phantom disappeared from the chair, and then Little Charlie waved goodbye, giggling into the distance until his voice was no more.

Harry was concerned for Clarisse and wanted to contact her, but he was confined in isolation for now; no means of communication or visitors allowed for the next couple of days.

The encounter with the phantom had sucked every ounce of energy from his delicate body. He was not ready for such a conversation.

Clarisse had two days remaining to conclude her agreement with the phantom. She was required to visit the cobalt chest two more times to ensure she had met her part of the deal. She felt apprehensive about another round of horrific encounters and needed to muster the mental strength to complete the task.

It was mid-week in Hartley, and nobody was staying at the Presbytery Inn. It would be a good time for her to gather herself and head down to the basement.

The basement felt surreal. All the sense of evil and darkness that shrouded the phantom was missing. It was like any other basement, except with a cobalt blue chest in pristine condition, polished with sparkle and a glittering exterior.

Clarisse followed her routine by unlocking the mortice lock then lifting the cover to see what awaited her inside. Gone was all the paraphernalia belonging to other people, such as the handmaiden's dress and Detective Hickes' cap. Instead, she found a straw, classic boater-style hat with a wide brim and ribbon. She placed the hat firmly on her head and adjusted it forward so it was well balanced.

Clarisse closed her eyes and was transformed into a prestigious horse racing carnival at Randwick Racecourse in Sydney. She was in the member's lounge with dignitaries from all walks of life, all dressed up in the most beautiful attire. Women pranced by with lovely gowns, and the men were tailored to the hilt in brand name suits of the highest quality.

People walked past her and smiled, making sure she acknowledged their presence. But why? It was as though she was a celebrity, a person of significance in society.

"Is there anything I can offer you, ma'am," asked a cocktail waiter who was fussing over her every need.

Next to him was the concierge, who stood there patiently abiding his turn for the cocktail waiter to finish.

"Are you ready to place a bet on the next race, ma'am?" he asked.

Clarisse was not sure what to say and had to act quickly. "Do you have a recommendation for me?"

"How about the favorite, ma'am, Virulent Desire? She is a new horse on the rise and expected to win."

"Okay, that will do. Good choice. Virulent Desire, it is," Clarisse said with a cheeky, affluent smile.

The concierge stood waiting, obedient, anticipating her next request. "How much, ma'am? Twenty thousand dollars like before?"

Clarisse's jaw dropped. She had never had that sort of money.

"Okay, yes, twenty thousand dollars on Virulent Desire for the win."

"Yes, ma'am. I also wish to inform you that your winnings from race one have been transferred to your account."

"Oh, thank you … And the winning horse's name again?" Clarisse asked.

"Miss Opulent, ma'am. The horse that won was Miss Opulent."

"Yes, of course … Miss Opulent. How could I forget?"

Clarisse sipped on the expensive, prize-winning red wine, a rare and mature cabernet sauvignon stored for many years in the restaurant cellar, reserved for important dignitaries.

"Ma'am, can I show you to your seat? The race is about to begin."

Clarisse made her way to the patron's section of the grandstand as people smiled and nodded toward her. She was not used to this type of attention, but she liked the glamour of being a celebrity.

"Your bet, ma'am." The concierge handed the betting slip to Clarisse. It was the 28th of March, two days into the future—race five, Randwick Stakes—horse number twelve, Virulent Desire.

Being witness to the future confused Clarisse as she had had only experienced horrible past events. Was this the power of the cobalt blue chest that the phantom had boasted about? The present, past, and future? The here, there, and everywhere? And whatever one wanted to be?

The day at the races ended with the final event before Clarisse returned to the cobalt blue chest and the basement room. She was feeling great after a couple of glasses of red wine and champagne. She had enjoyed the notoriety and people pampering her, something she could get used to.

She wanted to test the phantom's credibility. If it was a race in the future, and it was a real event, then she could win the races when the carnival was scheduled to take place.

Clarisse set up an online sports betting account, ready to place her trust in the Randwick Stakes. Race one was scheduled at eleven a.m., and the form guide listed Miss Opulent as one of the favorites to win the race.

Not wanting to use all her money at once, she placed a small bet on Miss Opulent for fifty dollars. If the phantom was right and could envision future events, then her chance of winning was assured—all the proof she needed to ensure the ghost was true to his word.

It was two days later and race day. Clarisse turned on her computer and logged into her betting account that she had created specifically for this event. She was not a betting person and had to learn quickly about horse race betting. The live streaming of race one was ready to go, and she held tightly onto her printed ticket.

*Miss Opulent*, she thought.

The race commenced at a frantic pace as the horses bolted in the 1000 meters stakes. It looked as though Miss Opulent was falling behind at the beginning and struggling to keep up with the other more fancied opponents. In a twist of faith, though, Miss Opulent caught up to the leading group as though afterburners were propelling her. At two hundred meters to go, she was in third place. The horse continued to drive herself forward with a massive effort—second place at one hundred meters.

Clarisse jolted with glee as Miss Opulent moved into first place with fifty meters left in the race and won. It was an impressive run as Miss Opulent won two lengths ahead of the second-place horse.

Clarisse had succeeded in winning race one of the Randwick Stakes, and her fifty-dollar bet had secured her four hundred dollars in winnings.

Her next task was to bet on Virulent Desire in race two. This time she decided to increase her bet to one thousand dollars. It was a large amount of money for Clarisse, but she was in the mood, confident her horse would win.

To kill time between race one and race two, she made a cup of coffee then waited patiently for the next race to begin. It was race two, Randwick Stakes, and Virulent Desire was the second favorite.

Clarisse felt a tingling in her stomach and was anxious about the outcome of the competition. One thousand dollars would land her four thousand dollars in winnings, according to the tote.

Clarisse remained glued to her laptop screen as the race readied, live streaming. She clasped her hands, and her legs shook uncontrollably.

The two thousand meters middle distance race started, and Virulent Desire comfortably settled in the leading group of horses. It appeared to be riding a strategic race and waiting to spring its surprise.

With four hundred meters to go, the leading group started to pull away from the rest of the horses. Virulent Desire was beginning to make its mark, moving into third place and narrowly behind the second and first place horses. With one hundred meters left in the race, Virulent Desire moved into second place and on the heels of the first-place horse—they were separated by half a length.

Clarisse was ecstatic and jumped out of her seat, preferring to watch the remaining part of the race on her tippy toes.

With fifty meters to go, Virulent Desire moved ahead into first place and started pulling away to win outright by a comfortable margin.

Clarisse had pocketed four thousand dollars. She placed her hands in front of her face and nearly cried with joy. She had never won a prize like that before.

And this was just a taste of what the phantom had to offer. He was drip-feeding her on becoming wealthy with all money she could muster and a place in society that made her feel like a princess—notoriety, exclusivity, with power and influence to boot. At least for the time being, she was captivated by the thought of a luxurious lifestyle if she accepted the phantom's terms after the five-day contract.

Clarisse left the basement, thinking, *What if I could win the lottery or make money on the stock market? I could take advantage of predicting rising property markets or invest in a start-up business that would turn into a game-changer and become a global company.* The prospects were endless, and her mind boggled at the thought.

## 12 THE KEEPER

Today was Clarisse's penultimate day of her contract with the phantom. She had seen the horrors of the dark side and the richness of the alternative. The ghost had complicated her decision by doing what any demon would do—find the weak spot and exploit it. Wealth, power, notoriety, and fame all came hand-in-hand for a princess. And why would you let go of that lifestyle once you had a taste for it?

Clarisse decided to go for a morning stroll around Saint Bernard's Church. Considering how long she had been in Hartley, besides the cemetery and the pond, she had never walked the grounds of the church to discover every nook and cranny. Perhaps today would be a day to explore the finer points that defined Hartley.

Clarisse made her way toward the front steps of the church, where she would commence her walk.

It was a brazen type of day as the clouds and sun played a standoff. One minute the rays of the sun warmed the back of her cardigan, and the next, disappeared behind the clouds to succumb to a mild breeze. She didn't know whether to remove her cardigan or leave it on, but that was Hartley—laid out amongst the hills and of a typical Australian landscape, it made the weather unpredictable.

As Clarisse walked amongst the crumbled leaves and uneven turf, she noticed a solitary figure in the background behind the vestry. He wasn't your typical-looking local—dark skin, white hair, and a skinny build typical of the indigenous people. His face was painted white in a powdered white paste, and his long, curly hair was tied back with a red headband. From afar, he looked mysterious, like a mystical character, as he pranced around, mumbling to himself. He was raking and brushing aside the leaves and branches from a plot of land approximately two feet in circumference.

Curiosity got the better of Clarisse, and she walked toward him, keen to find out who he was.

"G'day, miss. Nice day for a stroll?" he said with a strong Australian accent.

"Hello, sir. I was walking around the church grounds to find—"

"To find something interesting, I assume?" he interjected.

"Yes, I guess so. My name is Clarisse, and I have been

staying in town for four weeks and never stepped beyond the front steps of the church." Clarisse pointed to the presbytery. "I am staying in the Presbytery Inn ... I think I'm the only one there today."

"Oh yes, miss, I know that place." He put down his rake and introduced himself. "I'm Warrin and descendent of the Wiradjuri tribe ... I am the keeper."

"You're an indigenous man?"

"Yes, miss." He pointed toward the pond directly in front of them and the tall eucalyptus tree.

"You're familiar with the place?" asked Clarisse.

"That's sacred land. Generations of my family respected that site for as long as we could remember." He was balanced on one foot while leaning on the rake. "I am the keeper of memories," he said.

Clarisse was speechless and did not know what to say. "I have been learning the history of Hartley. Tell me more?"

"Sure, miss. My grandfather was Tracker Joe, and he worked for the constabulary, helping find people—murderers, thieves, and anyone else wanted by the law. But his biggest case was the missing priest—Father Grimaldi."

"He told you that story, too?"

"Yes, and others." Warrin stood silent for a moment. "Everything was peaceful for a while when Hartley became a ghost town. The spirits of the land found solace again … until …"

"Until what?"

"Paranormal Jack started his paranormal tours and aroused the spirits again. It made them upset and restless."

Clarisse absorbed his candid explanation. "Are these spirits with us now?"

"Oh yes, they have always been with us, miss, and unfortunately, brought other dark forces with them.

"You mean bad spirits?"

"No, miss. In your world, they are called demons."

Clarisse was silent, not sure how to react.

"We know about the phantom," said Warrin candidly. "And no … before you think about it, I'm not one of his concubines. I am a real person."

"You know about the phantom?" Clarisse reinforced.

"Yes?"

"And Little Charlie?"

"I know about him, also." Warrin pointed toward the pond again. "That's where he died."

"I assume you know Eleanor, the handmaiden," Clarisse said intuitively.

"I have seen her around the place sometimes. She comes in and out when we have visitors."

Clarisse was dumbfounded that Warrin knew about the

phantom's concubines. "And what about Captain Aldershot?"

"Oh yes, the man who started it all. He brought the demon here in his chest and started a spiritual war with the caretakers of the land." Warrin picked up his rake and started clearing the leaves. "You know, miss, some towns should stay empty forever. This town should never have been awakened."

"What brings you here, Warrin?" Clarisse asked.

"This very spot is a ceremonial place for my people. Your Captain Aldershot decided to build a church right next to it." He continued raking, more rigorously this time. "I am clearing it because it's our custom to keep it proper … respect for my people."

Clarisse was silenced as she stared directly at Warrin unknowingly. She wanted to know more, but at the same time, she lacked the courage.

"Has he offered you a contract?" asked Warrin. It was an inevitable question.

"You know about that, too?"

"My grandfather warned me about the phantom—his cunning ways."

"Yes, he offered me a contract for five days … then I must make a decision."

"He has gone soft on you, miss. He doesn't normally

offer a way out. Must be something new?"

Clarisse did not understand how Warrin was so informed about the phantom and his tactics. Nothing in Hartley should surprise her anymore. Something new was always withering around the corner.

"It's a pleasure meeting you, miss … Off to that yara tree; make it good and proper for the birrani—for the boy." He turned and started walking toward the tree. "Need to make it respectable for the little boy; tidy up the area, because no one else is looking after it."

"How do I get rid of the evil!" Clarisse yelled impromptu.

"You don't destroy the evil, miss; you outsmart it so it has no influence anymore!" Warrin kept walking then turned toward Clarisse. "His master, the evil one, he won't like it and will turn against him; pick him off, if you know what I mean. Just like he picked off the others before him."

Clarisse stared into the distance without a flicker of an eyelid. She could not believe her conversation with Warrin. Was it a coincidence or meant to be? Who knew?

She was not prepared to leave the conversation this way, so she decided to follow Warrin at a steady pace until she caught up with him, almost tripping on a branch directly in her path.

"So, how do I stop it?" she called out. Clarisse had a gut

feeling that Warrin was not letting her in on all the information.

Warrin turned around, startled to find Clarisse following.

"Tell me how I stop it!" she repeated.

"Look at the contract, miss," he said reluctantly. "Look inside the chest and make sure you haven't missed anything."

"I don't have a damn contract."

"Yes, you do, miss. Look in the chest—it's there." Warrin glanced at Clarisse again. "Read every word in the contract. I am sure he tried to trick you somewhere."

"You mean, he hasn't explained everything?"

"Ha-ha. He is the devil, miss; why would he explain everything to you? It's a game, remember?"

Warrin kept walking toward the eucalyptus tree to clean up the site. With a rake in one hand and a bin in the other, he disappeared behind the church.

Clarisse returned to the presbytery, agitated and perplexed. Her situation had become more complex, and there was more to the agreement with the phantom than she had anticipated. She was also angry with herself that she had let the phantom con her into thinking the contract was rock solid. It was like dealing with a used car salesperson or a real estate agent—some were dirty rotten.

She made her way down the stairs and straight to the basement. Clarisse was on a mission, determined to get to the bottom of her arrangement with the phantom.

This time, the cobalt blue chest was open and ready for her. There was no need to raise the lid and undo the rusty mortice lock.

She peered into the chest to find a document folded into three parts with a wax seal—the contract. Clarisse was so anxious to open it that she tore the side of the paper. It was two pages long and handwritten in old English-style typeface. Next to the contract was another document—an appendix. It was not in the envelope but detached in a different location.

Clarisse wanted to skim through the material, but that came at risk—the devil was in the details—so she had to slow down, reading word for word and sentence by sentence. It was an excruciating way to read a document when you were feeling ruffled and agitated. Her hands shook as she attempted to curtail her nervousness.

"Ah, there it is," she said. She carefully reread the sentence to make sure.

"Goddamn trickster," she whispered.

*If the person bound by this contract profits from the vision of the future by securing any form of wealth, on three occasions or more, they shall forfeit this contract.*

Clarisse had prospered from the vision of the horse races at Randwick. Her bets had landed her over four thousand dollars. If she prospered from one more vision, then all bets were off and her disclaimer voided, no get-out clause. She would be unable to lead a regular life again and become a prisoner to the cobalt blue chest and the evil that resided within.

If it weren't for Warrin, her life would have changed for the worst—unbeknown and captive to the nefarious that controlled all aspects of life in Hartley. However, Clarisse should have known better. What else had she expected from the phantom? Her naivety caught her out and had left her precariously close to giving away her soul. And even though Harry's life was guaranteed, it would have meant that she would never see him again. Her mortal life would have transformed into the keeper of the cobalt chest.

Clarisse folded the contract several times then tucked it into her front pocket.

Inside the cobalt chest was another piece of paper—a lottery ticket for this weekend's grand prize. She understood it was a plant from the phantom. One more strike and she was out.

Clarisse was not a keen lottery player and rarely purchased tickets. Her only knowledge of the lottery came through Harry, who occasionally punted with a system of numbers randomly chosen from his mathematical prowess.

She was done with the chest for today. One more day left on her contract and a final visit the next day would wrap it up.

Clarisse opted to spend the afternoon on the front porch of the presbytery, watching the arrivals for the weekend wedding ceremonies. There was always something about weddings that made them exciting spectacles—nervous grooms and frivolous brides with a harem of bridesmaids. It was more like a show than a ceremony as they all tried to outdo each other and take the spotlight. The days of simple traditional weddings had made way for stage shows and groomsmen forced to put on a dancing show.

Clarisse sipped on her tea while laying back on the two-seater. She removed the contract from her back pocket and unfolded it. She wanted to recheck it because the devil was in the details. As for the lottery ticket, she knew the rules. Even if she had the winning ticket and a multimillion-dollar prize to boot, she planned to burn it. She was not going to fall into the trap that the phantom had meticulously laid out for her.

While taking another sip of her tea and stretching out her legs, she saw an image of Warrin. White-faced with a rake in hand, peering through the shrubs next to the car park. He kept looking toward the car park as wedding guests continued to parade in.

Clarisse shook her head and rubbed her eyes to make sure it was him. She turned her head, and he was gone.

Warrin seemed to have a habit of popping up in places only to move on in an instant. He was shy and a recluse and did not like too much attention.

Clarisse thought about Harry and how much she missed him. She had the opportunity to speak to him on the phone the day before, and he had been upbeat about returning to Hartley in the next couple of days. However, he had mentioned the drugs making him hallucinate and recounted an apparition in his room taunting him. Clarisse had asked him who it could have been? All he could remember was the image of a sailor in a captain's hat. Harry had said the apparition was from a different generation, spoke old-style English, and called himself Captain Aldershot.

Clarisse had gulped when she had heard about Captain Aldershot, knowing it was the phantom taunting Harry in his hospital bed.

It was all a game for the phantom, so he had probably

gone to see Harry to poke fun at him, knowing she would eventually find out about it.

Clarisse had sidetracked the conversation with Harry and told him it was probably the effects of the medicine and nothing more, as he was on a potent cocktail of antibiotics and other painkillers. It was also what Harry had thought, so it had not taken too much convincing on her behalf.

## 13 THE STANDOFF

Harry was starting to feel much better. The doctor had removed the drip that supported his recovery, since he no longer required intense medication. And besides the usual headache and stuffy nose, he was feeling no further effects from the infection. He was looking forward to his return to Hartley in a couple of days and tidying up his project. His employer had already lined up a new plan for him—bigger and better as recognition for his success. Harry's career was on the up, and he was sure to leverage off his current assignment in Hartley.

The evening sun was starting to crest over the horizon, the bright rays filtering through the gaps of the worn-out window blinds. He became accustomed to the setting of the sun as nature's dial. It provided him with a sense of time without needing to look at his watch.

He turned to the side table to get a glass of water when he noticed the apparition of an old-style detective sitting in the visitor's chair. Next to the ghost was Little Charlie playing with his rope. He flung it around continuously like a lasso and smiled. Detective Hickes winked at Harry as he lit up his pipe.

Harry wasn't too sure if he was still feeling the effects of the intense drug treatment or whether the pathogen lingered in his mind, playing tricks and distorting reality as a side effect.

"Good evening, dear sir. You've made a great recovery. And don't worry; whatever happens to Clarisse tomorrow will have no bearing on you."

"What are you talking about?" Harry smirked in disbelief. "You're not real."

"Oh yes, I am. But think what you like. It makes no difference to me," said the apparition.

"So, why are you here?"

The phantom took a puff off his pipe then blew the apple-scented tobacco across the room. "I'm just fulfilling my contract, making sure you're recovering as planned." The phantom laughed then said, "If you don't recover, then the contract is void. Nobody wants that to happen."

"What contract are you talking about?" Harry was confused. The phantom was talking in riddles and was nonsensical.

"The one that you make with a devil. Not your usual

type of contract," said the phantom in a sarcastic manner. He took another puff off his pipe, and Little Charlie continued spinning his lasso.

Harry turned on his side and lifted himself upright to get a better view. "I don't know what you are talking about. Contract, devil, recovery? I think you're mad … whoever you are. Or maybe it's these fucking drugs!"

The phantom smiled and did not overreact, except for Little Charlie who decided to give Harry a round of applause, clapping vigorously with joy. The clapping echoed across the room as though he was in a theatre.

Harry lowered his head, placing his hands over his ears to reduce the decibels. When he raised his head once more, the phantom and Little Charlie were gone, and the room filled with the sun's rays again. He didn't quite understand what he had witnessed, but being the skeptic, he put it down to the infection and the cocktail of drugs. How else was he going to explain the visitation rationally?

"This is a nasty infection," he whispered to himself. He took a sip of water then set the glass back on the side table.

Clarisse made her way to the basement and the cobalt blue chest for the last time. It was the final day of the trial, and she was feeling jittery and uptight, wanting to get the whole thing over and done.

With every visit to the basement, one could not predict which angle the phantom was going to play. The anticipation of not knowing was what brought enjoyment to the evil entity. Watching her suffer from bouts of nervousness and disquiet; that was the game he played.

Her walk to the basement was effortless and with no precursor to navigate through this time. She had read in the contract that the phantom could not make direct contact during the five days, unduly influencing her decision making. However, that did not prevent the cobalt chest from radiating its dynamic chroma and intensity. The spiritual side of the chest was exempt and acted as a conduit to the metaphysical world.

As happened during her previous visits, the chest lid was open, waiting for her to partake in the next step. She peered into it, expecting to find some paraphernalia, but nothing. Only a card. And it wasn't any type of card, but rather a funeral service eulogy for her mother, Marlita.

Clarisse's stomach tightened, and she clenched her hand tightly, shaking it rigorously as tingles crawled up her arms. She was ready to burst into tears at any moment. However, the chest had other ideas, and she was flung into a hospice room.

The imagery was real, to the point that she could smell the stale hospital air and touch the visitor's chair. She rubbed her hands along the worn-out fabric and felt an immediate sensation creep up her body.

Marlita was lying in bed with a tube down her throat and unconscious. Next to her were monitoring machines that measured her pulse—*beep, beep, beep*. The stenograph in the monitor peaked up and down in tune with the beeps.

She wanted to cry and rush to her aid, but she could not move beyond the confines of the chair. She was stuck and helpless.

Clarisse punched and kicked the chair in anger, sending it flat on its back. Then she screamed to Marlita, "Mother! Mother, can you hear me!"

There was no reaction. Nothingness filled the void in the room.

Clarisse was at odds with herself as she felt the pain of her mother dying in front of her.

The beeping on the cardiac recorder was slowing down, and the graph on the monitor was starting to flatline.

"Mother! Mother, it's me—Clarisse. Wake up!"

But there was no point; Clarisse was shut off from the future and was not in the same dimension that her mother occupied.

Clarisse tried desperately to control her hard-felt emotions, needing to reason. She reread the eulogy and found a timestamp. It was fifteen years from her present time. The future was playing out in front of her.

"I can help your mother, my dear," a familiar voice reverberated throughout the room. It was the phantom intervening.

"You're not supposed to contact me, phantom. You know the rules of our contract." Clarisse was irritated by his presence.

"You mortals always like to throw the contract in my face when it does not suit you anymore," the phantom said, trying to be a know-it-all. "The contract excludes me from talking to you in the present, but we are in the future now."

"So, you found a loophole?"

"Ha-ha. I have always said you are the smartest of the lot—you catch on quick." The phantom was silent for a while then continued, "Let's cut through all the contract requirements and get to the point. I can save your mother; keep her alive for another twenty years, if you like. What do you say? Do we have a deal?"

Clarisse understood there was a semblance of truth about predicting the future, but winning horse races and lotteries were different from predicting the end of life for someone's existence.

"Well, do we have a deal or not? Do you want to see your mother die in front of you?"

"No, we don't have a deal!" The devil's contempt and

cynicism made Clarisse stronger.

Marlita's heart rate was declining and had set off an alarm on the ECG. The graph was flat-lining on the screen, and her breathing was starting to slow.

"One last chance, my dear ... What do you say? Save your mother?" The phantom was scoffing at Clarisse and toying with her.

"No! I said no!" Clarisse kicked the chair and sent it rebounding off the wall, leaving a gaping hole at the impact point. The phantom's shenanigans angered her, and she had lost her tolerance.

The phantom growled in anger, knowing he had a contest on his hands. Clarisse was smarter and mentally more hardened than the other concubines who he had conquered in the past.

The room shook from his disapproval as Clarisse tried desperately to maintain her footing. The faint image of her mother became blurred as a doctor and nurse rushed into the room to her aid. There was commotion as the hospital staff frantically tried to save her.

Clarisse reached out with open arms to find she had returned to the basement where she had left off. She had played the phantom's bluff but not without a personal impact. Her mother's pain resonated within her, disheartening her by the thought that she had nearly lost her mother while unable to offer support. It was excruciating not to be there in her dying moments.

Clarisse had completed her final visit to the cobalt blue chest. Now she had to decide this evening whether to accept the phantom's offer of wealth and riches beyond her dreams. Her contractual obligations were completed.

She wanted a stiff drink and badly. Not one to drink alcohol frequently, but under the circumstances, these were exceptional moments. The torment of experiencing her ill-fated mother's death was all too much for her level of tolerance.

Clarisse found a bottle of local red wine that had been left behind by the visiting triage of wedding parties, unopened and still with the cork. She helped herself to a glass in the dining room then made her way to the familiar porch overlooking the main street of Hartley. She needed to chill out and think, away from all the distractions. The patio and the furniture she occupied provided a getaway zone, a place of solitude and refuge. No one bothered her there.

She pulled out the lottery ticket from her back pocket. She could smell the wine's aromatic and fruity fragrance. It was a local brand that had won prestigious awards and carried a gold label stamp.

"Should I check the ticket?" she whispered, casting doubt on herself.

"But what if I have the winning ticket?" she implied again.

In a spontaneous act, she tore up the lottery ticket into tiny pieces and threw it into the breeze. She watched as the small pieces of paper were picked up by a swirling current and thrown among the shrubs, glittering as they reflected the sunlight.

From what had become a moment of heartfelt pain had turned into a show of encouragement; nature's way of reconciling the fact that she had made the right decision and had conquered greed and lust.

Clarisse's time had arrived, and she was ready to deliver her answer. Accept or not accept the phantom's terms? She decided to communicate her decision on the steps of Saint Bernard's Church, away from the influence of the basement and the cobalt blue chest. She thought the setting would provide her with a metaphysical advantage over the predominance of the phantom.

The backdrop was surreal. Behind her was the cemetery of departed souls lying in peace over generations and scorned for their decadence. In front of her, a monument that stood for hope and enlightenment to the settlers of the area. It was the Lord's house that brought the faith and God's words. If you stood behind the decrepit fence line of the cemetery, facing the front of the church, all you could see in front of you was a misty sapphire haze and the rough outline of the church's façade.

It was late in the afternoon, and the temperature had dropped significantly. There was a chill in the air that penetrated your bones, but no breeze. It was dead still and frozen in time. It felt as though nothing moved, and they were caught in the moment.

"Are you here to give me your response?" asked the phantom.

"It does not say in the contract where I should deliver my response to you?" Clarisse was firm. She was not in the mood to succumb to the phantom's senseless attitude.

Clarisse performed a full three-hundred-and-sixty-degree turn but could not detect where the phantom's voice was originating. She looked again through the misty haze to find his faint outline hovering in front of the church, just before the steps to the entrance.

"My decision is no. I don't accept your terms," she said forcefully.

The phantom was quiet. That was not what he had expected.

"So, you don't want the riches that await you? The

power, influence, and notoriety?"

"No, I don't, phantom." Clarisse was confident in her reply. "You tried to trick me in the last vision with the impending death of my mother. How could I trust you after that?"

"So, you brought Warrin with you to support your case?"

Clarisse looked to her side and saw Warrin peering from the shrubs adjacent the church. He was white-faced and standing on one leg as the other rested on his knee. His distinctive red headband was holding back his curly, long white hair.

"I didn't know he was here. Does it bother you?" Clarisse asked innocently.

"He neither bothers nor frightens me. It's not the first time I have dealt with his kind."

Although the phantom was shrugging it off, Clarisse had a gut feeling that Warrin's presence irritated him.

"So, are we done, phantom? My answer is no."

"My dear, I am the devil, and we are never true to our word. I make the rules and break them. I was having fun with you with the five-day discretionary clause, appeasing my master, if anything. I never really meant it."

"Because it's a game that you conjured up to make your master happy?" asked Clarisse.

"We don't need to talk about my master. It's simple from here on. Your darling Harry will fall sick again and die from the mysterious pathogen."

Clarisse stood tall, gallantly, and with zeal. She was not giving in to his antics. "I think we do need to talk about your master, because he forbids you to change the terms of the contract."

"How would you know?" the phantom asked. He was not as cocky as before, and his sarcasm had waned.

Clarisse smirked. "I have an appendix to the contract, a new clause that forbids you to change the terms."

"Where did you get that from?" The phantom was in a rage.

"From the same blue cobalt chest I got all the other paraphernalia." Clarisse crossed her arms defiantly. "I believe your master wanted to complicate the game and hold you accountable for the five days, add a new twist to your frolic and enjoyment."

"What do you mean?"

"If you could not convert my allegiances within five days, then you failed and not me. All bets would be off, and the contract voided." Clarisse threw the appendix onto the ground in front of her. "Have a look for yourself."

The phantom was silent for a moment. Clarisse could hear Warrin in the background, chanting as he played the sticks and slapped his thighs. It was a rhythmic sound and dance that blended into the surroundings, a call to the sacred land.

"I am the devil, and I own this land—I make the decisions," said the phantom. He was in an uncontrolled rage as his voice echoed throughout the cemetery and bounced off the tips of the eucalyptus trees.

The appendix that lay on the muddy ground in front of her caught fire spontaneously as it whirled in a circular motion until the papers were no more.

Clarisse bided her time and said, "Your master has many of you in towns all around the world; you said so yourself at our first encounter. He may gain some and lose some of you. It's all part of his game."

"You think he will give up this destitute place to that man and his spirits?" The phantom pointed at Warrin.

Next to the phantom stood Eleanor the Handmaiden, Detective Hickes, Father O'Leary, Father O'Hara and, finally, Captain Aldershot. The ghost did not take the form of the devil and opted for the image of Father Grimaldi. There they stood, all his concubines in a straight line, looking haplessly toward Clarisse.

"The final decision rests with you, phantom. You either honor our contract or you don't." Clarisse was firm in her response, knowing she was playing a high stakes game. "If you don't, you become powerless and have no hold on all the souls you have stolen over the years."

Warrin raised the intensity of his chant as the corroboree reached for the stars. Embers from the ritual fire that encircled Warrin filled the air in a spiraling display of yellow hues and strikingly bright orange-red sparks.

The apparitions realized they were free at last; their souls released from the reins of the phantom. He had lost his power and could not hold onto them anymore.

One by one, the apparitions disappeared into the darkness with a burst of light. First, it was Eleanor, then Father O'Leary, followed by Father O'Hara. Detective Hickes, Captain Aldershot was the last to go.

Little Charlie appeared immune to it all. He turned around and walked away into the bush. Clarisse wanted to give chase and bring him back, but Warrin raised his hand and looked directly at her. He sensed it was not the right thing to do or the right moment. Clarisse stood firm and followed his lead—she also had a hunch it was best left alone.

Once all the concubines disappeared into the darkness, the phantom had nothing left, bereft of his limitless powers. They were his tools of the trade, and he could not be powerful without them.

He let off one giant roar that shook everything around

them as a gaping hole opened from the earth below, fire and brimstone pulsating through the cracks. The fire swirled like a twister and swallowed him up, sucking his soul into the depths of the underworld.

The embers from the fire that radiated around Warrin spun furiously. They made their way into the sky and to the eucalyptus tree next to the pond.

The phantom was on his way to the fires of hell. The spirits of the land had reclaimed Hartley.

Harry and Clarisse stepped into the car that was fully loaded with their belongings.

"Ready to go?" Harry asked.

"Not sure if I am going to miss this place." Clarisse smiled.

Harry looked at Clarisse then reversed out of the car park and onto the main street of Hartley.

Clarisse glanced toward Saint Bernard's Church one more time as they said farewell to the place where so much had happened.

As they drove past the old police station, Warrin waved goodbye as he held onto his Jack Russel. Harry was oblivious of what was going on around him, stepping on the accelerator.

Clarisse could not help turning around to view the

Presbytery Inn one more time. She blinked more than once, unable to believe what she was seeing.

Little Charlie, in his grubby grey shorts and long socks, was waving goodbye from the porch as he held onto his bloodstained rope. He grinned continuously until they were out of sight.

Clarisse swallowed. It was not over. She felt Little Charlie's taunt. His innocent poise was a camouflage for the evil incarnate.

### The End

## ABOUT THE AUTHOR

Janice Tremayne is an Amazon bestselling and award-winning ghost and supernatural writer. Janice is a finalist in the Readers' Favorite 2020 International Book Awards in Fiction-Supernatural.

Janice is an emerging Australian author who lives with her family in Melbourne. Her recent publication, Haunting in Hartley, reached number one in the Amazon kindle ranking for Occult Supernatural, Ghosts and Haunted Houses categories hot new releases and bestseller.

She is well-versed in her cultural superstitions and how they influence daily life and customs. She has developed a passion and style for writing ghost and supernatural novels for new adult readers. The concept of writing the Haunting Clarisse series was spawned over a cup of coffee many years ago and she has never looked back since. Her books contain heart-thumping, bone-chilling, and thought-provoking ghost and paranormal experiences that deliver a new twist to every tale.

Visit Janice's website to learn about the next book in the series.

www.janicetremayne.com

Made in the USA
Columbia, SC
28 April 2022